T0116945

The Stranger From The Valley

Oscar William Case

iUniverse, Inc.
New York   Bloomington

The Stranger From The Valley

iUniverse books may be ordered through booksellers or by contacting:

iUniverse
1663 Liberty Drive
Bloomington, IN 47403
www.iuniverse.com
1-800-Authors (1-800-288-4677)

ISBN: 978-1-4401-6615-0 (sc)
ISBN: 978-1-4401-6616-7 (ebk)

Printed in the United States of America

iUniverse rev. date: 8/11/2009

CHAPTER 1

"Why you dirty ole rascal, you," he said, and jerked his head back, but not far enough to evade the wicked right crunch on his jaw that sent him turning to the side and lifting his hand to the welt on his cheekbone. "Yow! That hurt! But, I'm going to make you pay for it you dirty son-of-a-gun."

The other man gave him a dirty look, and replied, "You little pipsqueak! It'll be a cold day in Hell, if you think you can whip me! Come on and get some more of that medicine, if you think you're man enough!"

Without saying another word, the "little pipsqueak" came in a rush, both fists whirling round and round before they let loose a barrage of blows direct to the midsection of his opponent.

"Oof! Unh! A-agh!" uttered the "dirty ole rascal," as he tried to protect himself, but receiving some blows to the stomach and knocking some of the wind out of his sails. "Oo-of! You darn... I'll get you for that!"

"Dirty ole rascal" pulled back to catch his breath, then sent a mighty left jab straight to the right side of the chin of the "little pipsqueak," causing the man to stop short in his performance with both hands hanging limp at his sides, and his eyes in a squint. With a shrug of the shoulders, the man said, "Stop! You win for now, but I'll get even with you, if it's the last thing I do," and held his jaw in his right hand.

"Any time you're ready, and from now on stay away from my house! If I catch you nosing around there again, you'll live to regret it."

The "dirty ole rascal" was Calvin "Cal" Fedderson, a local resident and hard worker. He was tall, slim, and good looking, according to the local women. Married, with four children and a pretty wife, he usually minded his own business and was hard to anger, would rather laugh than throw a punch at somebody.

"But, on this warm summer day," as Cal explained it to me later, "I was irrigating a hayfield north of town a couple of miles when the little pipsqueak came by on the nearby road walking along behind his team of horses that were all harnessed up like he was going somewhere important. He saw me out in the field by myself and thought that this would be a good time to teach me a lesson. His name is Roger Proudmire, a short, cocky man with a large head, small in the shoulder, broad-chest with his stomach starting to bulge under his overalls, older than me, and married to my wife's sister.

"Since my family moved into this little town, I noticed he had taken an interest in my wife, talking with her every chance he got, then shutting up when I came close, as if he and my wife were planning a rendezvous somewhere. But, Barbara, my wife, would always tell me afterwards what he was up to, since it was her sister's husband being so forward. And, of course, I would tell my friends about it, hoping the message would get back to him.

"But, I haven't told anybody about his surreptitious visits to the home of the local widow, who had a son out of wedlock and is known to make great oyster stew. He explained to me that these visits were for charity purposes to deliver the poor lady some things out of his garden or some canned goods or a bag of flour, etc., for the church welfare, of course, since she had no means of supporting herself and son.

"I would rile him up on occasions of family get-togethers when I would catch him alone, by asking him what he was really doing over at the widow's house after dark.

"He would always tell me that he was delivering welfare goods for the church, but don't go blabbing about it, you know how the church likes to keep those things quiet. Then he would give me that holier-than-thou look with intense anger showing in his eyes, and try to get my wife alone again.

"Anyway, I watched him walk back to the road, a little lopsided from the blows, almost falling down as he climbed through the barbed wire fence. He was almost through when he started to straighten up, and his shirt caught a snag from one of the barbs and was hanging on to him like a hook in a fish's mouth. He started cussing and tore the shirt, scratching his shoulder as he pulled away. He turned around and gave me a dirty look, as I laughed at his predicament. He untied the reins from the fencepost where he had left them and slapped them down hard on the horses' haunches, causing the animals to jump and take off like a shot out of a civil war rifle, dragging him along as fast as his short little legs could run, and causing me to laugh so hard I had to hold onto the shovel I was using.

"I knew that this wouldn't be the end of it, but I wasn't going to lose any sleep over it. He would probably brag to his wife about how he had taken me in a fight, and I would learn all about it the next time Barbara and the girls went down there to visit with her sister."

He paused and took a deep breath, turning his blue eyes to me for just a second, and let out his breath in a long sigh.

"So, now you know the story about me and that ole son-a-gun, Roger. He just didn't know when to leave well enough alone, if you ask me."

"What about the widow? Do you know much about that?"

"Well, not too much. I've been told that she's the town hussy. Men are always dropping in to her place for one reason or another, maybe one or two a week and old Roger stops there to deliver his welfare goods, at least that's what he would tell me. Her boy was always outside playing. Whether he was sent out by her or just went out, I don't know. I've seen him out in the snow and cold with just a sweater on. He's probably five or six years' old. I guess she has to get some money somehow."

"How long has she lived here? Did she have the boy here?"

"I never thought about that. I just assumed she was a long-time resident, and as far as I know, the boy was born here. You know, I haven't been here too long either. I could find out, if you think you really want to know."

"Uh, no, not necessary, I don't think. I'll pay her a visit and have a chat with her. So, have you had any squabbles with anybody else around here, or is that the only one?"

"I get along pretty good with about everyone else. It's a friendly town, as long as you don't ask too many questions. They change the subject, if you get too personal."

"Well, I better be running along. Thanks for talking to me. Do you know which house is Henberry's, J. Henberry's?"

"You bet, but he doesn't live here in the town proper. His house is out on the Six-Mile Road near his mill. He runs an old grist mill out that way. You can't miss it, once you get on that road. There's a house on the corner, as you turn on to the road, and his is about six or eight miles further, the only other house out that way. It's been nice talking with you."

"Maybe you better tell me where the widow lives. If it's in town, I might go there first, and catch Henberry some other time."

We had been carrying on this conversation on the front porch of his house. We made ourselves comfortable on the two wooden chairs he told me he had made when they lived down in LePorcherie and couldn't bear to part with them when he moved up here. They were not exactly to my liking, but were sturdy and well constructed for their purpose with arm rests, ideal for the porch or about anywhere outside, too big and clumsy for a living room or kitchen.

"If you come over here and look around the corner of the house, you can almost see her place behind the schoolhouse," he said, as he got up and walked along the porch to the side railing.

Following him, I looked around the corner of his house where he was pointing. In the distance I could see the old wooden schoolhouse, but that was about all, except for a couple of wooden buildings on the corner of the road that ran behind the school from our viewpoint. Those buildings were about a quarter-mile from the schoolhouse, and looking directly at the school, I noticed another small building peeking out from behind.

"That little building sticking out there by the school is one of her outbuildings. Her house is just a few yards from there, but you can't see it from here," he said, lowering his arm to his side. "It's actually about a quarter-mile away from the school on the other side of that road that runs up to the creek."

"I should be able to find it pretty easy, it looks like. Thanks again."

And with that I returned to my horse, mounted, gave a wave to Fedderson, and started the short trip to the widow's place. I killed the time by talking to Spottie, my horse. "We're sure not making any progress on our purpose for coming up here, are we Spottie? How did I get sidetracked? We don't have to get to it 'til the Fourth anyway, so we might as well look around and get to know these people, especially the two we're interested in, huh, Spottie?"

Spottie turned his head around and went "huffle," and gave a grunt in assent; at least I took it as that.

I turned north at the corner by the two wooden buildings. They looked pretty rundown. The windows on the side facing the road were all broken, like some kid had tossed rocks through them. There was no fence, so I directed Spottie to the side of the building nearest the corner where I could gape through the window. The room inside was empty with the floor boards broken in a couple of places showing black holes, and the wall opposite had some of the plaster missing, exposing the laths. Glancing through the open door in the wall into the other room, I saw an old man with a grayish-white beard sleeping in a chair, his shirt off, and his suspenders running over his underwear, his beard resting on his gray, hairy chest. At least I hope he was just sleeping. I urged Spottie back onto the dirt road and continued to the widow's house.

Tying Spottie's reins to the gate post, I walked up to the front door and knocked three times. A boy came running around the corner of the house, went directly to the horse and patted him gently on the nose.

"Be careful there! He might take a nip out of your hand!"

"Gee, mister, that sure is a pretty horse," he said, walking toward me. "My Ma ain't home."

"Well, young feller, do you know when she'll be back?"

I took a good look at him as he gazed first at me then Spottie. He was a fairly average looking youngster, somewhat scrawny with brown unruly hair, in overalls and torn shirt, barefooted, but it was a warm day. His bony kneecaps were peeking through the holes in his pant legs, where they were worn out.

The boy shook his head up and down, but didn't say anything, looking at me with a "give me something" look. I dug in my front pocket, pulled out two pennies, and held them out for him to take.

He grabbed the pennies and informed me that, "Ma'll be back 'bout sundown," and scampered around the corner of the house in the direction he had emerged.

I started back out to the fence to get on Spottie and try the Henberry place, when I heard the door open behind me, and someone said, "Are you looking for me?"

"The youngster told me that you weren't home," I said, returning to the small porch.

"Yes, he tells everybody that, but you can see, here I am. How can I help you, mister? It ain't suppertime yet, so you can't be wanting something to eat. That's when the men usually stop by."

She wasn't an unattractive woman, around 40-45, some wrinkles on her cheeks from smiling too much, I thought, some more visible on each side of her black eyes, could be part Indian from her features. She was still slim, and not as tall as I was, coming up to about my upper chest. Her black hair hung down just below her shoulders.

"No, no, I'm not hungry, but I heard you make a good oyster stew," I said, smiling. "I just came to talk with you a mite, if I may. I'm Chappie Wesford, and am just passing through your town talking to some of the residents. I live down in the valley."

She looked at me closer, to make sure I wasn't lying or something, then pulled the neck of her black and green dress up a little, even though it covered her shoulders and chest pretty well, looked me square in the eye, and said, "Come in and close the door to keep out the flies."

I took a quick survey of the inside, as I stepped through the doorway. There wasn't much clutter or mess in the front room, a couple of pillows on the settee, and four chairs scattered around with a small table to one side, two pictures on the wall ahead, one, a painting of her, I supposed it was she, and a man dressed in a suit coat. She saw me staring at it.

"Eddie Jensen did that. That's me and him, he told me. So I hung it on the wall, he was so proud of it. He called himself an artist, but I don't think he paints people very good. I sure don't think she looks anything like me. What do you think?"

"I recognized you right off. That's you, all right, but it doesn't quite look like he finished it. He lacks a little something. Color, maybe, in the faces. But I don't know anything about painting pictures."

She led me into the kitchen and told me to have a seat at the table.

"I'm going to make a pot of tea and we'll talk. My name is Esther Bigknife. I was married to a Ute some years ago. He got killed in a mine accident over in the mountains," she informed me, as she took the pot off the stove and filled it with water from a bucket sitting on the stand in the corner, then placed it back on the stove. She added a couple of pieces of coal to the small fire in the stove. But the room didn't need the extra heat, as it was pretty warm already.

"This won't take long to heat up," she announced, putting four teaspoons of green tea leaves into the water from the package she took from the small cupboard. "I hope you like tea. I do, especially in the afternoons." She replaced the package in the cupboard and took the chair opposite me.

"Well, what did you want to talk about? And is that all you want to do?" she asked, raising her dark eyes to look at me.

I ignored the second part, and asked her, "Where did you move from to settle in a small town like this?"

"Before I married Charlie the Ute, I was married to another man who had dreams of owning a ranch and raising a herd of cattle, and so we came here from Kansas....Kansas City. He had put all his money in cattle, and we homesteaded a section out to the east of here. Of course, he didn't know anything about the cattle business and we ended up losing everything to the bank. One day he said he was going to go look at some land up north a ways, not to worry about anything, he'd be back before sundown. When he didn't show up for two or three days, I asked Roger Proudmire, who was our nearest neighbor then, to go look for him. It wasn't like him to be gone for so long. Roger found him all right, and brought his body back to me. Roger said he found him up in Skunk Pass with the gun still in his hand." She let out a long sigh and looked at me with sadness in her eyes. "And that's about it. I found this little house and moved to town, since I didn't have any place else, and married Charlie after a few years."

"The boy, is he Charlie's or the other feller's."

"Yes, he was born about a year after I married Charlie. I think he looks a lot like him, too."

"And I guess Mr. Proudmire stepped in to help you out after Charlie's unfortunate accident?"

"Well, a year or so after, Mr. Proudmire started bringing me some food items, from the church, he said. He had been selected by the Bishop to serve on the welfare committee, and he started dropping off things here, mostly for the boy's sake, he said. He didn't approve of what I was doing, so he always said it was to help out the boy."

I watched her as she talked. She would look at me when she started, then look away, usually at her fingers or maybe across the room at something, then move her pretty eyes back to me, and smile just a little. She arose and moved the boiling teapot to a cooler part of the iron stove, reached in the cupboard and took down two cups and sat them on the table. Returning to the cupboard, she removed two saucers and brought them back to the table, arranging the cups smartly on them with her long, slim fingers. She then poured us a cup of green tea, sat down, reached for the sugar bowl, which was already there, put two heaping spoonfuls into her tea, and slid the sugar over to my side of the table. I could see why the men were stopping by. At times, she was outright pretty with her strong, slim body moving smoothly with no effort, it seemed to me. She appeared younger than I first thought.

"We became friends. I felt sorry for him, I guess. He started telling me all his problems at home, and I would console him, and tell him what I thought about it. And he'd leave the groceries and stuff, and go on home."

"What kind of problems did he have, that he had to tell you about, that he couldn't talk over with his wife or other family?"

"I shouldn't't've told you that. It was a private matter and he didn't want anybody to know. I don't know why he told me, but I will say it was about money, partly. And that's all I can tell you."

"I'll drop the subject, and you don't have to tell me, anyway. Did you and Roger have any type of romantic relationship, if you can call it that?"

She stared at me for a few seconds, trying to read my thoughts, glanced at her fingers. She returned her eyes to my face and continued.

"Well, uh, no. We never got involved in that way. I know you may have heard about me, because everyone seems to know what goes on in my life or at least think they do, but it isn't that way. He was just fulfilling his duties for the church, and that was as far as it went other than our little chats. That's all."

"This is a small town and everybody knows everybody's business, I guess. Do you know the Henberrys?" I said, changing the subject.

"Not directly. I've seen them in church, but I don't get involved in the other meetings, so I don't know them very well." Somehow, she didn't sound very convincing, as she gave me a quick glance. "That's about the only time I see them, except for the elder Jim. I see him at the cheese factory occasionally. Why?"

The boy came bursting into the kitchen, coming directly to the table, and asked his mother if he could have a cup of tea.

"Now, Charlie, you shouldn't be interrupting us, but sit down and I'll pour you some tea."

He sat on the other chair at the table, stared at me, as his mother retrieved another cup and saucer from the cupboard, strained some tea into his cup and added some sugar.

"Would you like some more, Mr. Wesford?"

"No, ma'am, but it sure hits the spot. Ain't that right, Charlie?"

"Yes, sir, it sure does," he replied, running his tongue across his lips and taking a sip from the cup. "It needs more sugar, Ma. You only put in one spoonful."

She looked at him with a scornful eye, and gave him a bit more.

"Well, Charlie, after we drink our tea, how would you like to take a ride on Spottie?" I asked.

"You bet! I would like that a lot! But, Ma don't let me ride on horses, yet. She says they're dangerous for boys." I noticed the excitement and disappointment in his dark eyes, as he looked at his mother.

"Maybe if I tell her you can ride behind me and hold on tight, she'll let you. What do you think Mrs. Bigknife? I think he's big enough to start learning to ride, myself."

"I just don't want him to get any big ideas about getting a horse, because I can't afford it right now, and Charlie's a little young to take care of it," she said, glaring at me and looking at her son through softened eyes. "Maybe just a short ride will make him know he's still too young. I guess you can take him up the road and back, if you make sure he doesn't fall off."

"Let's finish our tea and go for a ride, Charlie," I said.

"Oh, boy, thanks Ma! I won't fall off, no sir," he said with enthusiasm, getting up from his chair and running out the door yelling at me to come on.

Mrs. Bigknife was smiling broadly as she looked at me and stood up.

"It looks like you may have a friend for life. Nobody ever offered to do that before, not even Mr. Proudmire when Charlie would practically beg him to let him just get on one of his horses for a minute. Thank you, Mr. Wesford, for bringing a little joy into his life."

"Shucks, no thanks required, Mrs. Bigknife, I'll be the one that has the most fun. You can bet on that," I said, walking to the front door.

She followed me out to the gate and watched as I climbed aboard Spottie and reached down, took Charlie by the arm and swung him up on the horse behind me.

"Put your arms around my body and hold on tight, Charlie. We'll go up to the creek and back, if that's all right with your mother."

"Go ahead. The creek is not very far," she said, looking up at us and exposing her slim white neck to the sun. She raised her right arm and shaded her eyes as we galloped away, Charlie hanging on for dear life.

Mrs. Bigknife was still outside when I returned with Charlie. Watching her as we approached, the way her body moved with the dress, her arms hanging at her sides, her hair hanging down on each side of her face on which was a big smile, she looked more attractive then before, if that was possible.

I swung the boy down next to his mother, and he took off running through the fields to tell a friend about the horse ride, excited as could be.

She yelled after him, "You get back here before sundown, Charlie!"

Staying in the saddle, I told her, "I may come back in a day or two, Mrs. Bigknife. I better get on over to the Henberrys before it gets too late. Thanks for the tea."

"That was awful nice of you to let Charlie take a ride. And come back any time, Mr. Wesford."

brim on his hat, which was dark gray, darker than the upper side covered in the flour. "I'm Jim Henberry, the younger. Who might you be?"

"Nice to meet you. They call me Chappie, Chappie Wesford from down in the valley."

We shook hands just as a shot came whirring by my head. Dropping to the ground and crawling for cover, Henberry by my side, I looked through the bushes in the direction I figured the shot came from, but there was no further activity along that line.

"I think he's gone by now, but I'm going to go see if he left a trail," I told Henberry. "I'll see you up at the house," and not waiting for a response, I jumped up and ran over to Spottie.

A half-hour later I was knocking on the Henberry's front door, as the sun sunk over the mountains leaving the little valley in the dusk and near dark.

"Come in, come in. Jim will be back in a minute. He's out in the barn cleaning some of the flour dust off his clothes. I'm Mrs. Henberry."

Stepping into the front room I noticed that Mr. Henberry had made his appearance, coming in from the door opposite, which I surmised lead to the kitchen. There was another door on the left.

"And this is the elder Jim, my husband," she added. She was not a tall woman, a little on the heavy side, with average looks, in her fifties.

"Come in, young man, and have a seat there on the settee. My son told me what happened down at the mill. Did you find anything?"

He was a large man with big hands with his belly pushing out the front of his overalls. His hair was turning to gray from black, but he appeared to me to be a serious type; he hadn't even smiled yet.

"Afraid not, Mr. Henberry," I said, shaking his hand. "By the time I made it across the creek, he had made his departure, or he could still be hiding in the thick undergrowth on the bank. It was getting too dark to see much, so I just came on up here."

I made myself comfortable as I could on the small couch, and continued, "I just wanted to talk to you a bit about a gent named Proudmire, Roger Proudmire."

"Well, I heard there was a stranger nosing around town asking questions, so how can I help you, Mr. ...uh ... Mr. ...."

"Wesford, Chappie Wesford."

"Yes. How can I help you, Mr. Wesford?"

"How long have you known Mr. Proudmire?"

"He and I go back a long way, practically to the founding of this town, twenty or thirty years ago, probably. A few years back, he was the first Mayor, and I thought he did a good job, but he lost in the next election. He volunteered to fight for the north in the War, but hasn't said much about it since he returned. As far as I know, he's always been an upright and respected citizen. Is he in trouble?"

"Do you know of anybody that had it in for him?"

"I don't get around much to talk with anyone, just the church meetings, and I've never heard anything there that would reflect on him in a bad way. He is very active in the church. I think he's trying to become the Bishop again." He looked at me with a stern, steady gaze with his green eyes. "As far as the mill goes, he brings his grain here to be ground into flour, like most of the town, but my sons, Jim, Oakley, and Milt, take care of the business there, now. I'm more of a homebody these days, ain't that right Maisie?"

"Uh-huh." She was sitting in the other easy chair across the small table next to the man of the house, with a needle and thread, fixing a shirt button. She raised her light-brown, grayish haired head and looked at me with a smile on her reddish lips.

Which led me to think, "He's probably just the opposite of that?"

The son, Jim, and another rough-looking character came into the room from outside. They both glanced at me then Mr. Henberry, then back to me, and Jim said, "We're all done for now, Pa. We're going to fix us something to eat, since you got company. C'mon Milt, let's go eat."

"Ain't you going to wait for Oakley?" Mrs. Henberry asked.

"Nah, he went to town to do some flirting with the Fedderson gal," replied Milt, keeping his eyes on me. "I think he's got the eye for her, for sure," and he laughed.

Mr. Henberry laughed, too, but the Mrs. uttered a sound like "tut-tut."

Milt was black-haired with dark features, while Jim had brown hair and a lighter complexion. Jim takes after his mother, Chappie thought. They didn't appear much different in age, only a year at the most.

"Now, where were we, Wesford?"

"I think I've about finished for now, I better be heading for town before the sun comes up, and let you folks get on with your supper. It's been nice talking with you, Mr. and Mrs. Henberry."

"I'll see you to the door," offered Henberry.

He followed me out to the porch and closed the door. "You don't think that whoever fired that shot was aiming at my son, do you?"

"I don't know why anyone would be taking target practice at either one of us, unless Jim has gotten himself into a mess. I certainly haven't, that I know of."

I turned and headed for my horse at the hitch rail, but Mr. Henberry followed me. "Jim's been a lot of things, but he ain't no crook," he said with finality.

I climbed on Spottie, looked at the man standing there in the dark, and told him, "You'll have to have a talk with him."

"I will, I will," he said as I waved so-long and started on the road to town.

I traveled over a couple of hills and directed Spottie to head up a side canyon, and when I thought I was sufficiently secluded, I dismounted and hunkered down to wait for Oakley Henberry to return home.

I didn't have to wait very long. I could hear him singing from a half-mile away, so I mounted Spottie and returned to the road, and acted like I was just taking a leisurely ride back to town. He was still singing loud and out of tune, but stopped in mid-lyric as he saw me in the moonlight a couple of hundred yards away. He kept coming, and I didn't change my horse's pace either. As we drew within 20 yards or so of each other, he pulled on the reins of his horse and came to a halt, saying, "Howdy, stranger. Going to town?"

"Might be, Oakley. Get all your courting done so early on this beautiful moonlit night?"

"Who the devil are you, mister?" he asked, moving his right hand from its hold on the reins down to the six-gun hanging from the belt, as I came up even with him.

"I wouldn't do anything foolhardy, if I was you, Oakley. I just been chatting with your folks, and they told me you were in town, and who else would be going to the Henberry place this time of day?"

"Well, you're right about that, mister. I'm Oakley, all right, and my courting didn't last too long tonight. She said she had something important to do, so I just turned around and headed home."

I took a good look at him. He was maybe eighteen or nineteen years old, broad in the shoulder, slim, and quick to smile with his white teeth showing in the moonlight beneath the shade of his hat brim. I asked him, "Is that Milt feller actually your brother, he looks entirely different than you and Jim do?"

"I reckon he is. He's been living with us as long as I been alive," he replied with a good laugh. "Shucks, mister, who do you think he is, if not a brother?"

I laughed too, "Just wondered, is all. Do you know a Proudmire, Roger Proudmire?"

"Everybody around here knows him. Mr. Proudmire's been living here a long time. Why, he was the Mayor when I was just a tike, and he was our Bishop some time before that. Why?"

"Have you seen him around town lately, or when was the last time you happened to see him?"

"You sure do ask a lot of questions, and I don't even know your name. What do you want to know about Mr. Proudmire for?"

I acted like I was adjusting my bedroll behind the saddle, ignoring his query, giving him a minute or two to adjust his memory.

"I don't rightly remember exactly when I saw him last. Could've been three, four months ago, I guess. He hasn't brought anything to the mill for awhile now, but the grain hasn't come on good yet."

"If you happen to remember, just leave word with the Feddersons for Chappie Wesford. I'll be around for awhile."

"The Feddersons, huh? I think I can do that."

I urged Spottie to a lope, and we were soon out of sight, if Oakley was watching.

Continuing on to the outskirts of the town, I turned southwest on the road to the valley to an isolated area that wasn't fit to grow anything and too bare and hilly to let the cattle loose on, although there were a few scattered cedar trees. I found the camp I had set up earlier far enough away from the road by a small stream and hidden behind the hills that no one would accidentally stumble upon, and made myself comfortable for the night under the stars.

I awakened from my deep slumber before daylight and had a cup of coffee and some hardtack before I saddled up Spottie for the ride back into Altaveel. The town's name was shortened and corrupted by the early local citizens from the French "Alpageville," and was called "Altveel" by most of them, but it got put on the maps as Altaveel. It was on top of one of the many foothills of the High Uintahs on fairly level ground, although swampy in spots, ideal for growing just about anything in a short summer with lots of space for cattle to roam and forage near the Ute Reservation. Although the Frenchman who first settled there and opened a small trading post for trade with the Indians arrived before the Latter Day Saints, the townsfolk were mostly Mormon now. The Mayor filled an honorary position, because most of the people always consulted the Bishop with any problems relating to the town proper. I think the mayoral election was a fairly recent innovation of a few people who had a desire to wield power of some sort, their egos going unrecognized in all the farming and cattle-raising. Anyway, I guess it was time I got around to talking with the Bishop a little bit. He should know more about what's going on around here than about anybody.

I went over the hills, concealing myself through the use of the sparse cedars as best I could and came out on the road about four miles further away from town where two hills came almost to the roadway. I didn't care if someone saw me get on the road this far away from my lone camping spot. I could always tell them I was taking a shortcut from the valley.

Urging Spottie to a lope for a ways, we slowed to a steady walk. No use getting to town too early. Give the Bishop time to open his store and make a couple of sales. This being Saturday some of the farmers would hitch up their wagons and load up their wives and kids for a day in town for some needed supplies and visiting with friends and relatives, a time-honored custom.

Entering town, I saw there was only one wagon with its team of horses hitched to the rail in front of the store. There wasn't anything else stirring on the main road that runs through the town, except some lady out in back of her house hanging clothes on the line to dry. I could see the Bigknife place and the two buildings on the corner of the road to the creek, and nearer to the store I could see the shell of the old hardware store and blacksmith shop. Next to that was the town stable run by old "Cranky" Cramer and a small tavern which I haven't had the privilege to visit yet and frowned on by the Bishop and some of the citizenry. I knew Cranky from when he lived down in the valley, and he thoroughly deserves the name. A more contrary man, there's never been. If you say a turnip's white, he'll say its green, the only color that it could be, he would argue, since the tops are green, the turnip has to be green. It was no use to argue with him. Leastways, that's the way he used to be.

I tied Spottie to the hitch rail, went into the store and stood in front of the candy case poring over the sweet concoctions while Bishop Thorneycraft tended to his one customer who seemed to be having trouble making up his mind which kind of ax to buy, double-headed or single.

"It don't make no difference, Zophar, you can only use one side at a time, anyway," Thorneycraft said, hoping Zophar would take the more expensive double-headed type.

"I know that, Thorney, but if I buy that two-headed one, I won't have to sharpen it so often, but it's a little dear for me just now."

"Your credit's good, and you got a good crop of wheat and barley coming on. I'd take that one, if I was you."

"My wife said to get some black thread and a bag of flour today..."

My mind came back to the candy case, then I wandered to the rear, and pretended to look at a saddle and some blankets, until the customer finally made his purchases and left.

"I didn't think he was ever going to make up his mind," said the Bishop, coming back to see what I was doing. "He took the single-head ax, the old skinflint. What can I do for you?"

"I'll take a couple pieces of that hard candy up in front there, and I'd like to talk with you about a couple of people, if you don't mind. I'm Chappie Wesford from down in the valley, Bishop Thorneycraft. You may have already heard of me."

"Yes, you're that feller been nosing around here asking questions for the last few days. Figured that was you when you came in. How can I help you, Mr. Wesford? And what gives you the right to be checking up on our church members, anyway? Between you and me, I was told that the reason for your visit was something else entirely."

"I know, everyone's wondering about that, but let's just say it's an official matter, and let it go at that, although I do want to know who took a potshot at me and Jim Henberry last night. But, I wanted to talk to you about Roger Proudmire and probably Calvin Fedderson. I heard Mr. Proudmire was an upstanding Mormon, so maybe you can tell me about his relationship with the church, Bishop."

"He's been a member for a long time, and right now he's head of our welfare department and doing a good job, too, I might add. He was the Bishop here once, and said he wouldn't mind doing it again. He's always been willing to help out when asked, even if it's to help clean out the church building when the regular janitor is unavailable for some reason, serving sacrament, collecting tithes, etc. Yes, sir, Roger's a big help around here, if you ask me, and I wouldn't be surprised if he doesn't end up Bishop again."

"Would you say he's honest? Has he ever stolen anything from the church that you know of?"

"Of course, he's honest as the day is long, and I've never known him to take anything that doesn't belong to him. He borrows things on occasion, but has always returned them. Why? Do you think he's a crook?"

He gave me a look like I shouldn't be asking him such dumb questions, and waited for me to answer his query. I looked him up and down, observing his well-worn black suit and string tie with a pair of old cowboy boots to set it off. He didn't want to appear too prosperous or the citizenry would start traveling to the valley to do their buying, even if they had to be on the road for four or five days going and coming. They were funny that way.

"What about Mr. Fedderson? What do you think about him?" I asked, instead of answering him.

"Hm-m, that Fed's a strange sort, married to the sister of Roger's wife, he is. Roger told me that Fed's got some kind of a grudge against him for some reason. He never explained why. He came in the store late yesterday with a black eye, and told me that that blankety-blank Fedderson had provoked him into a fight when he was going to help out ole man Lupadakis get his wagon out of the creek. Wouldn't put it past Fedderson, no sir. He's a newcomer to town, and it takes awhile to fit in."

"How long's his family been living here?"

"Only about three, four years."

"What was the wagon doing in the creek in the first place?"

The Bishop looked surprised at that question, and then relaxed as he told me. "Oh, that's right, you wouldn't know. That wagon's been in the creek ever since Mr. Lupadakis ran off the bridge going home in an inebriated state one night and broke his leg. He was lucky that was all that was broke and got out alive. The creek was running high from all that rain we got, and he shouldn't have tried to cross that bridge. It was partially underwater and got washed away with the wagon on top of it."

He looked at me to see if there was any reaction to his story, but not hearing anything, he continued, "I've heard say that the Lord looks after those not in their right minds, and He did in this case. That ole drunk barely escaped from being swept away, too. The wagon was half-buried in the mud as it got swung around to the creek bank. The horses were able to break away and get out on their own, but George was thrown down in the bed of the wagon and twisted his right leg enough to break it, his foot being caught in the floorboards. He's a lucky cuss, all right. Everybody in town heard about the accident, and most of them went out to take a look, including myself. Mr. Proudmire volunteered to get the wagon out when the water went down. No one else cared enough to help the town drunk."

Thorneycraft gave Wesford another inquiring look to see if there was a reaction this time, but not getting one, he continued.

"Roger told me yesterday, that the wagon was almost freed. One more day of digging should do it, he said."

"Does his family sit by the Fedderson's in your church meetings?"

"Of course, when both of them attend. Their wives like to catch up on family news and such. Fedderson usually manages to sit in another group, though, and sometimes by himself."

"Where is that bridge that got washed away?"

"About three miles west of town. If you take the road by the creek you can't miss it, because the road turns north there and used to cross over. With the creek running low now, we get along without the bridge. The next one we build will be longer and stronger."

Another customer came into the store, a family with the wife and three kids along. I walked back to the candy case following Mr. Thorneycraft, and Mrs. Thorneycraft came in from a door in the rear.

"How do you do, Mr. and Mrs. Bourne? Nice day, isn't it?" Thorneycraft greeted them.

I stared into the display to determine a piece of candy I might like, as the three young ones watched me, the youngest probably three years old. "I think I'll get a piece of horehound, what do you think?" I asked the one standing next to me.

Mrs. Thorneycraft went behind the counter as she greeted the Bournes, "Good morning, Liza. My, your family's sure growing up fast."

"They sure are. Can't keep them in clothes, they grow so fast. I'm going to look at some fabric back there, Jane."

"You go right ahead. Just yell if you need some help."

The kids were looking over every piece of candy in sight with eyes wide open, but not saying anything. Finally, the one next to me announced her decision,

"I like that peppermint drop, right there! I don't like horehound!"

"I do!" the oldest boy exclaimed. "Boys like it."

"I'll take some of this candy, Mrs. Thorneycraft," I said. "Give me three horehounds and a peppermint drop."

"Will that be all for you, mister?"

I gave her enough money for the candy, then gave each of the kids a piece and stuck one in my mouth watching the big smiles on their faces.

"Gee, thanks, mister!"

I left the store, hopped on Spottie, and went to take a look at the mired wagon, thinking that Proudmire would be there digging again today. The sun was shining on the trees and bushes along the banks of the creek, with some clouds way low on the horizon to the south. One the north and west the mountains loomed bright and colorful, still some snow on the highest peak up to the north. I let Spottie set the pace, and we took our time reaching the wagon. I could hear Proudmire yelling from a half-mile away, where the creek made a turn. There was not much water running in there today, maybe a foot deep in the deepest places, but it was too wide to get much deeper than five-six inches as it tumbled over the rocks and around the boulders. As I came nearer to the bridge area, most of the water ran into the bank as it made a curve to the northwest, and it may have been two or three feet deep there. Where the bridge used to be was about two-hundred yards further on and another fifty or seventy-five yards to the partially buried wagon.

Proudmire was there with his team hooked up to the wagon tongue. I had heard him yelling back there, but now he was quiet, sitting on the bank, sweating, wondering what he was going to try next, and watching me approach.

I crossed the stream to the other bank where he was sitting, and asked him if he needed any help.

"I've about reached my wit's end trying to get that thing out of there. I just about had it, and then it rolled back. You got any suggestions?"

"Let me look around a bit."

Working together, we soon had the wagon sitting on the creek bank.

"By golly! That did it! Finally! I owe you a debt of gratitude, mister, and I don't even know your name. Ole Lupadakis's going to owe *me*, though, after all that work! By golly!"

"Chappie. Chappie Wesford's the name, Mr. Proudmire."

I gave him a closer look now that the work was finished. We were both leaning against the freed wagon like it was an old friend. His dark face was smiling under his beat-up felt hat. He had black hair, bushy black eyebrows, a bulbous type nose, black pupils in the eyes, creases in his cheeks around his mouth, and a couple of missing teeth under a bruised eye and jaw.

"I've been wanting to talk with you, Mr. Proudmire, if you don't mind. The Bishop told me that you were the only one offering to help get the wagon out 'cause Lupadakis wasn't much liked by anybody, and I took a ride out here to gander at the mired wagon."

He stared at me for a few seconds, like he had never seen me before, and he hadn't.

"I heard somebody'd been looking for me asking a lot of questions. What do you want?"

"I hear you been working on this for a week or so. It must've been pretty well buried."

"Well, he's a pretty cranky ole cuss, ole George is, and he drinks too much, making it worse, but I always got along well enough with him. He treats the Henberrys like dirt when they grind his grain. I don't know how they put up with it. Even I can't stand his ranting and raving at times. The Bishop's glad he's not a Mormon."

"What do you think about Calvin Fedderson? Do you know him well?"

"I don't think much of him, but I am married to his wife's sister. That dirty ole rascal gave me this bruise on my face. He just hit me out of spite. I had gone out in the field to help him out, and the first thing you know, he threw a punch at me. He told me to stay away from his place, like I don't have a right to take my wife to visit her sister."

"How long they been married?"

"Not as long as I have. They were already married for quite awhile when they moved here. They only been here for a couple years, and he doesn't fit in very good with the townsfolk. I've heard some of them talking."

"You wouldn't be having designs on his wife, would you?"

He gave me a funny look with fire in his eyes and clenched his hands into fists, then threw a roundhouse right at my jaw.

I ducked under it, grabbed his wrist, and gave it a twist that turned him around, and held it against his back between his shoulder blades, his belly up against the sideboards of the wagon.

"No need to get belligerent, Roger! It was just a simple question."

"I...I... It's none of your business what I do, but, the answer is shucks no. Whatever gave you that idea?" he grunted.

I released his arm, saying, "You got to learn to control that quick temper, Mr. Proudmire. It might get you hurt next time."

He didn't say anything, but he was facing me now, breathing a little heavy, and was ready to take another swing, until he saw the look in my eyes. He took a deep breath and relaxed.

I asked him, "When's the last time you been out by the Henberry mill?"

"I don't go out that way very often," he said still staring at me, "unless I'm getting some grain ground or going hunting or fishing, or to chop some wood in the mountains." He took another deep breath. "I guess it was three, four weeks ago to get some more firewood. What's that got to do with anything?"

"Did you ever run into Fedderson while you were in the mountains?"

"No. Never did, except the first time the wife's family had a reunion over there. Wasn't long after the Feddersons moved onto the hill," he replied, fully relaxed and friendly now. "We all got together and spent a few days camping and swapping tales, etc. That's the first time I met him. He was kind of quiet, didn't say much. Went off with his kids and left Barbara talking to her relatives. I felt it was my duty to at least escort her around with my wife until he returned. When he finally got back and heard about it, he was terribly upset, came after me threatening to break my neck."

"When he hit you, had you threatened him in any way? I heard he's slow to anger."

"Heck no. I just offered to help him finish his irrigating was all, and he just hauled off and cracked me a good one."

"Esther Bigknife told me that you were the one that discovered her husband's body a few years ago. How friendly are you with her?"

"Not friendly at all. I just deliver her some welfare goods once in awhile. I heard that she's not a very moral woman, but she attends church pretty regular," he told me, quickly glancing away.

"How did you find that body? I heard he committed suicide up in Skunk Pass."

"He did. One morning, Mrs. Briggs, Esther, came a-visiting in a state of high agitation all worried about her husband. She asked me to go up there and see if I could find him and tell him to come home. She needed some work done around their place. So I saddled up ole Bronco and put some supplies on my mule and headed up there. About four miles into the canyon, I saw his horse with the saddle still on him along the trail eating some grass, but I couldn't see him around anywhere. Riding around the area, I saw the body in a little side canyon. Since we don't have no law around here, I loaded old Brigg's body on to his horse and brought him back to their place. And, since I was the Mayor then, I sent Dale Sideburn to Valleycrest to notify the Marshal. And that's how it came about.

"By the time I got to the Briggs' place there was some blood coming from the wound, since his head was hanging on one side of the horse and the feet on the other. It was a pretty messy sight, and I'm sorry that the widow had to see it. As it was, I didn't find him 'til late in the afternoon, and didn't get him home 'til about 10 o'clock that night."

"Don't the Marshal have to hold a hearing or something when something like that happens?"

"He sure did. It took three or four days for him to get up here after he was notified. He told Dale Sideburn he had some other business to take care of first, but when he finally got here, Briggs had been cleaned up and dressed in his best suit, and was in the church waiting for the funeral ceremony to start. The Marshal saw him lying in his casket, and made a note about the hole in his head, and told them to proceed with the burial. He hung around 'til after he was put in the ground, then he asked me a few questions, then Mrs. Bigknife, or Briggs, and the next day we rode up to the place I found ole Briggs at. He took a look around, then we came back to town, and he went on back to the valley. At least that's where he said he was going, and I haven't seen him since. I guess that's what you mean by a hearing isn't it?"

"I guess so. Who is Dale Sideburn?"

"He's the feller we sent to tell the Marshal. Dale was going down that way, so Thorney and I asked him to notify the law when he got there."

He looked me in the eye, smiled, and shook my hand. I watched him climb on one of the horses, and head north on the road.

CHAPTER 3

I sat on the bank watching the water sliding and gurgling over the rocks and ate some jerky from my small supply in the saddle bag, thinking I would go take a look around the Henberry mill in the daylight. Maybe I could find something that would lead me to the person who shot at us last night. I finished my jerky, climbed aboard Spottie, and headed for Six-Mile Road.

I turned off the road before I reached the mill, and crossed the river to the mountain side where there was sufficient cover. I didn't particularly want to be seen by the Henberry brothers, or anyone else, for that matter. Walking through the trees and bushes on the river bank, I took another look around for any trace of the person who took that shot at me, but, whoever it was had made a clean getaway, leaving no tracks, spent cartridges or anything else.

But, why would anyone want to get rid of me, or was it Jim they wanted to kill?

I returned to where I had tethered Spottie, climbed onto the saddle, leisurely went back across the stream the way I had come, and rode up to the front of the mill.

"I see you came back a little earlier today. Want to see where we grind the grain, huh?" Young Jim Henberry said when I entered the dark place. He didn't seem at all concerned that he had been shot at. Did he know who the shooter was?

"Sure and a few more questions," I replied.

"Let's go look at the grinders first, then we'll talk. Through this door here are the large stones, and the farmers drop off their grain at the loading dock there. We haul it through this door and put it on this elevator here and hoist it up there, where it is dumped into the hopper. The grain falls through the hole in the middle of the top stone and is ground as it whirls around on the bottom stone. The flour falls out on the edge and is carried around where it falls through this hole and into a bag. And, there you have it," Jim yelled over the noise of the pulleys, belts, motors, and grinding stones.

We walked outside where it was considerably more quiet, brushing the dust off our hats and clothes, and we could carry on a normal conversation.

"That's a noisy operation, if you ask me, and no wonder you get covered in flour dust, it's all over the place inside there. I've always wanted to see what goes on inside a mill. If it wasn't so noisy, I might try to find a job in one for awhile. I've heard tell that they're not too safe, though, from all that dust floating through the air, a spontaneous explosion could blow the mill to Kingdom come. Have you ever heard of that?"

"My father told me about that when I was younger. That's why we have to shut her down ever so often and get rid of all the stuff in the air. Some days the wind doesn't blow through there, and we have to shut her down 'til it clears out. Milt operates the machinery down below."

"Yah, I saw him down there. Was he working yesterday evening when we were talking?"

He gave me a dirty look and smiled, "I don't know what you're getting at, but if you think Milt was shooting at us, you got another think coming."

'What was that other brother, Oakley, doing? I ran into him on the road after I left."

"As far as I know he was in town flirting. Left right after lunch. He figures himself quite a ladies man, being the youngest and all."

"Does he work in the mill?"

"Sure does. He's the one dumps the grain into the hopper. But, like I said, business is kind of slow now."

"How often do you and Milt go into town?"

"Well, tonight's the Saturday night dance at the church. Other than that, I go into town whenever Pa tells me, but I sure do like to dance. That Milt spends most of the time in the saloon when he goes to town, or at that Widow Bigknife's place, which to my mind is pretty often."

I tried to picture Milt with Esther, but no matter how hard I tried, I just couldn't conjure one up. I just couldn't get a good mental photograph of him and Mrs. Bigknife; she seemed so entirely the opposite of that crude, ugly brute. I'll have to talk with her again. It just doesn't fit.

"Does the whole family go to the dances, or just you and Milt?"

"Oh, we all go, it being at the church. That's where Oakley met that Fedderson girl. You should give it a try, since you seem to becoming a fixture around here," he chuckled.

"Maybe I will. Maybe I will. Is your father home now?"

"Nah. He and Ma always go into town on dance Saturdays to visit and see what's new at ole Thorneycraft's store."

"Been nice talking with you. Maybe I'll see you later on."

"If you go to the dance, you will for sure, Chappie."

Leaving there, I took the Six-Mile Road back to town, thinking that I hadn't found out much about the shooting or much else for that matter. Interesting little settlement, though. Poking along the road with the day beginning to get dark and letting Spottie set his pace, something on the road behind us was demanding my attention. Turning around, I saw three horses just coming around the hill I had recently passed about a half-mile back. It had to be the Henberry brothers heading for the dance, so I pulled on the reins and waited for them to overtake me. Oakley was out front of the other two by about fifty yards, but he didn't slow down as he went barreling past, yelling, "Come on there stranger, let's get to town before it gets any darker!"

The other two Jim and Milt weren't in so big a hurry that they couldn't stop and say hello.

"Howdy, there, Chappie," Jim greeted. "You're sure taking your time. Why I took a dip in the creek to clean off the flour dust and put on my dancing clothes, already, and you're still on Six-Mile Road. You been snooping around some more?"

Milt had his hand resting on the butt of the pistol hanging in the holster from his waist, looking at me like I was some kind of spoiled food he had just pushed away, but not saying anything.

"Ain't in no hurry to get where I'm going, Jim," I said keeping my eyes on Milt. "Did your brother here change into dancing apparel, too?"

"Nah, he don't take to dancing, do you, Milt?"

"C'mon, Jim, let's get going. My throat's getting parched from all this talking in the flying dust," said Milt, staring at me. "What's he care whether I'm going dancing or not?"

"I don't care, not a whit, 'cause I don't plan to ask you to dance," I said with a loud laugh, looking at Jim. "Your brother Milt just don't appeal to me, and besides, I'm not much of a dancer myself."

Milt pulled the gun out of its holster and aimed at my chest, "You don't appeal to me none, neither, stranger, and anymore talk like that will get you a case of lead in the chest, won't it Jim?"

"Take it easy, Milt. He was just making a little joke, is all. No use getting all riled up at that, is there, Chappie?"

"Why, shucks no, just a little humor, is all. It's like a man climbing up in a tree to take pot shots at something he could just as well shoot at from a foot or two away. Don't you see the humor in that, Milt?"

"I don't know what you're talking about, but your little jokes ain't too funny. Who's climbing trees to do their shooting?"

"Don't rightly know, do we Jim? But somebody last night took a shot at Jim and me from one of the trees across the creek. Any ideas who?"

"Could be any number of people the way you been nosing around, but it wasn't me. I heard the shot, too, but it ain't unusual." He re-holstered his six-gun, seeing that I wasn't going to react to his anger. "A lot of people come out here to go hunting and such, especially the younger ones. C'mon, Jim, you're going to miss all the dancing, if we don't get a move on."

"See you boys later, then," I said, as they resumed their outing.

That Milt is a cantankerous sort and gets riled awful easy. Yet, he seems to possess a modicum of rationality, I thought, as I urged Spottie on toward the settlement. "C'mon, Spottie, let's go see what that dance is like!"

After I turned off Six-Mile Road, I could see a wagon and two or three men on horseback up ahead in the near dark heading to the dance, too, I assumed. When I came near the church, Cal Fedderson was helping his wife down from their buggy. They lived close enough they could've walked to the church, but chose to ride in the buggy for some reason.

"Howdy, there, Cal! Do you mind if I tie Spottie to the back end of your buggy? It seems to be pretty crowded around here tonight!"

He responded with a wide smile showing his white teeth, "Go right ahead, Chappie, then I'd like you to meet Mrs. Fedderson. My two girls have already run into the dancehall."

They were both middle-aged, about my age, I thought, as I finished tying the reins and taking a good look at the

Mrs. She was not as tall as her husband, of course, with her dark blond hair in a knot under a bonnet and wearing a clean muslin dress with a flower print. She certainly was not what I would call ugly, smiling at me with her slim mouth and blue eyes. She held out her hand as Cal said, "Ma, this is Chappie Wesford, the fellow I was talking to on the porch a couple days ago."

"Nice to meet you, Mr. Wesford," she said, as she gave me a handshake like a man.

"It's all my pleasure, Mrs. Fedderson," I replied, gently squeezing her big hand and smiling. "Cal told me that you and Mrs. Proudmire are sisters."

"We are. Have you met her?"

When I shook my head to indicate that I hadn't, she said, "Let's go inside, and I'll introduce you, won't we Calvin?"

"You two go ahead. I want to talk with Mr. Henberry over there," Cal replied, and pointed to a small group walking toward the church from a house down the road. It was dark by now, and how he knew they were the Henberrys was beyond me. He wanted to avoid Roger Proudmire, if he could.

At the entrance was a sign placed on a wooden tripod which read, "For Tonight All Weapons Prohibited Including Guns, Brass Knuckles, Clubs and Other Dangerous Articles of Mayhem. Please Leave Them Outside!"

After the dance was over, it was easy to see why so many people attended. For this night, Bishop Thorneycraft had arranged for a musical group from the valley to come and play for the locals. There were a piano player playing on the church piano, a violinist for the waltzes, who also played the banjo, a trumpet player sounding the notes of Moroni, an accordionist, and a fiddle player for the square dances and old Irish folk tunes.

If I had known about that, I wouldn't have been there, for I was well acquainted with the fiddle player, being his brother, and the real reason for my being in town might be exposed. However, it wasn't my brother who disclosed it, but the Bishop himself, having learned of it before I even arrived in the town. At least that was what I thought might occur. But, it didn't happen. The only person who said anything about it was Thorneycraft, and that was to me. Ted, my brother, was too busy playing fiddle and flirting with the young ladies to do much talking at all before I had a word with him.

As the dance was drawing to a close, the Bishop took me into his office in the church, and told me that he knew why I was here, and would have talked to me about it when I was in the store, but said he couldn't because of the other people there. The only place he knew he couldn't be overheard was right here, in the church office. "I didn't want to do any disservice to anybody by spreading rumors around, since I had been told not to say anything. And, if I can do anything to further your job, just let me know."

"I appreciate that, Bishop, especially not telling anyone," and with that being sufficiently covered, I changed the subject to something more mundane. "Could you tell me about the cheese factory here in town? It doesn't have anything to do with why I'm here, though. Do the Henberrys ever bring any cream or milk to be made into cheese. They own some dairy cows, don't they?"

"Oh, yes. Old man Henberry owns the factory and hired George Calderson to run the milk and cheese operations for him. All those cows in that field around the factory belong to Henberry. You might stop in there and take a look around. It's interesting, if you never seen cheese made."

"I'm not too interested in cheese-making, but I will take a look just for the heck of it. Was that it on the road there just south of town? That building with the big doors and a loading dock?"

"That's it, all right," and he looked at me with a look that said, I don't know whether I should ask this or not. But, he did. "How long do you think it'll be before you return to the valley?"

"Can't tell you for sure? Maybe another week or two, maybe less, maybe more." I peered into his brown eyes and asked, "Does Fedderson and Proudmire ever bring any milk and cream to be made into cheese?"

"Proudmire does. Fedderson only has one or two cows. He works for the Indians and the school. He doesn't seem to like the thought of running a dairy herd. Besides, that piece of land he owns ain't big enough to support much, and it's too swampy."

I was going to ask him questions about the relationship between Milt Henberry and his brothers and Esther Bigknife, but there was a knock on the door. There was something about them that just didn't set right, but I would have to ask him later.

"That'll be the janitor telling me it's time to close up the church. Do you have any more questions?"

I did, but I said, "Nah. Nothing I can't ask tomorrow or the next day."

It had been a grand old dance in the Western fashion with a lot of participation in the square dances, but less in the waltzes. The young, single farmers and ranch hands took advantage of this night of sociability, dancing with any of the single women who showed them any sign of interest, whether good-looking or not. The younger boys and girls were running around the dance floor having a good time, some even attempting to imitate the adults in the waltzes, and really enjoying the special square dances where they were given the floor to strut their moves. Most of them were shuffled off to the stage area by nine o'clock to catch some sleep while the adults took over the dance floor. I even had a couple of dances with Mrs. Fedderson and her sister, and one with her daughter, Hilaine, when she got away from Oakley, all very enjoyable.

"This is getting to be more work than fun anymore," Ted told me as we were waiting for the other musicians to finish loading there equipment onto the old stagecoach they had borrowed for the trip up to the foothills. "Those old farmers and their wives sure enjoyed the music, though. Everybody was smiling and having a good time."

"I don't imagine they get to hear good dancing music like you boys produce very often, so it's a real treat for them," I told him. "By the way, I appreciate you not saying anything about my trip up here."

"That's all right. I know better than that. When you coming home? Ma's worried about you, even though you are old as Methuselah," he laughed. "She worries about every little thing that comes along. If she doesn't have nothing to worry about, she ain't happy."

"Tell her I'll be back in a couple of weeks, and I'm fine, and enjoying meeting all the Altaveel folks."

"C'mon, Ted, we're waiting for you!" one of the musicians yelled from the coach. "We got a long ride ahead of us!"

"Hold your horses, I'll be right there!"

We shook hands, and he climbed into the coach. The piano player was sitting on top of the coach in the driver's seat, and he yelled, "Haya! Haya! Giddy-up! Giddy-up!"

CHAPTER 4

I watched the coach disappear down the road into the night, but could still hear the driver urging his animals on, "Haya! Haya!" and finally that died out, and there was almost complete silence, except for the noise coming from the saloon down the road.

I retrieved Spottie from the hitch rail where he had been moved, and leading him toward the saloon, I walked the quarter-mile to the local watering hole. There were four or five horses waiting patiently in front for their owners to reach their sufficiency in alcohol.

Tying Spottie's reins to a fencepost a few yards to the side, I left my artillery in the saddle bag where I had stowed it earlier, and entered the tavern, that is, after three drunk cowhands staggered through the door and out to their horses, one losing his grip on the saddle horn as he was trying to get aboard and falling to the ground yelling, "Whoa, there, Brownie! Hold her steady, there!" and laughing uncontrollably as he reached for the saddle horn again, "Whoo-ee, everything's moving. Ha-ha-ha, whoo-eee! Upsa daisy, there! Ah-ha, that's it Brownie! Away we go, now, giddy-up! Ha-ha-ha-ha!"

"You're drunker than any sick dog I ever did see. Just don't get sick and throw up all over the sagebrush again, Willy? Ha-ha-ha!" one of his companions encouraged, as they raced off into the dark.

"Well, lookee here, look what the polecat drug in!" Milt Henberry said, looking at me standing just inside the small room, the only other customer. "Cranky, pour old Chappie a beer for old time's sake! I ain't seen him for a couple of hours!"

"Funny, Milt," I responded. "I thought you'd be over at the Bigknife place by now. It's almost midnight."

He gave me the dirtiest look he could configure his face and eyes into, and said, "Buster, what might you mean by them words? Them's enough to cause a feller to get a broken jaw or worse. Where I am at midnight's nobody's business, especially any of yours." He was standing at the bar with both fists clenched, ready to take a swing at me.

"You're right, Milt, It ain't none of my business," I said as Cranky placed the glass of beer on the bar. I lifted the glass and looked Milt in the eye, saying, "I don't much care about drinking to old times. How about let's drink to Widow Bigknife and little Charlie. Now there's something I could drink to about every day."

"Why you..." Milt took a step closer and let loose a long right that would have caught my jaw for sure, if I hadn't ducked under it and threw a powerful right of my own into the short ribs on his right side as he continued on around from the force of his blow. My punch knocked the wind out of his sails and bent him over hitting his head on the bar and effectively putting him out of action.

Cranky came around the bar with his arm held high holding his shillelagh ready to crack my skull, saying, "What'd you do that for? He's my best customer!"

"Hold on there, Cranky! And put that club down. He's the one started this. I was just making polite conversation when he took a swing at me."

He slowly lowered the club, but said, "You better get out of here, because when he wakes up, he'll be gunning for you."

"He wouldn't shoot an unarmed man, would he?"

"He ain't too ethical, he don't care if you got a gun or not."

He was going to continue talking, but the door swung open and Jim and Oakley entered the tavern. Seeing Milt lying on the floor, Jim asked, "What happened to Milt?"

"I guess he drank too much, too fast. He fell and hit his head on the bar," I answered.

Cranky gave me a nonchalant stare and went back behind the bar with his club. "Why don't you boys take Milt home. You, too, Chappie, better make tracks before he comes around. He might not remember what happened, and take it out on you."

"That's all right. I want to parley with you in private as soon as they clear out," I replied.

Oakley drew his gun, pointing it in my direction, saying, "You heard him. Better clear out of here before he gets awake. Milt's meaner than a grizzly, if he thinks he's been tricked or something."

Jim broke in, "Put that thing away, Oakley, before you get hurt, too. You heard Chappie say he wants to talk to Cranky, and I'm sure he will. Let's take Milt home. Grab his feet, and I'll get him under the arms."

Milt was starting to fuss and moan, putting one hand to his head as Jim started to lift him up.

"He's waking up. Just let him come around on his own, and we'll see what happens," I said.

"Hey, Milt, it's time to head home," said Jim. "It looks like you been drinking pretty heavy. Some fresh air'll do you good. That's it, get up slow."

"Ugh, what happened? My head hurts terrible," Milt groaned. Spotting Cranky looking at him from over the bar above, he seemed to remember where he was, "What in hell did you put in that last drink, Cranky?" Looking around he spied me and sputtered, "Is...Is...Are you still... here? I took a swing at you, you lousy soddy, for talking about Esther, and then I blacked out. How long ago was that? Jim...Jim, I think I owe him an apology, 'cause he didn't mean anything by it. The liquor got to me, I guess. Help me up, and let's get out of here."

"That blow on the head must've done something to his mind. You're a lucky feller there, Chappie," the bartender was saying after the Henberrys cleared out. "I just about swung my club at your head, too."

"Lucky, all right, if you say so, Cranky, but let me ask you, how long you been here in town?"

"I got to close up the place. The church let's me stay in business only as long as I close by midnight and don't cause any trouble for anybody. Let me put these lamps out, and we'll go in back and talk."

I watched him lock the front door, blow out two of the lamps, and take another one down from its nail.

"Follow me," he said and led me through a door near the bar, down a short hallway, and into his living quarters. He placed the lamp on the only table, said, "Have a seat," and sat down on the other chair. He immediately got up again grabbed the lamp, saying, "I'll be right back."

I sat there in the dark listening for any sound coming from the bar as Cranky did what he went to do. In a couple of minutes he returned with the lamp and two mugs of beer carried in one hand by the long handles on the sides of the glasses.

"I like to have a little nightcap after closing up. Care to join me?" he asked as he sat down.

"Don't mind if I do."

"Ah-h-h, um-m, that tastes good on a parched throat. Now where were we?" he queried, after taking a big gulp of the beer. "Ah, yes. How long have I been here? Let's see. I guess we've lived here about eight or ten years, but we've owned some property over there to the east a ways, down in Muddy Basin, so I'm fairly familiar with the people around here. Never had any trouble, even though I'm supposed to be an obnoxious, cranky feller. I'm cranky all right, 'cause all these devout religious meddlers been trying to drive me out of town, or at least close up my livelihood. Who wouldn't be cranky? By the way, that's the first fight I ever had in here. The ranch hands get awful drunk on occasion, but I've never known them to fight each other. You must've touched a nerve in ole Milt. He usually drinks by himself and nobody bothers him. Why do you suppose that is?"

Did he mean, did I touch a nerve or that nobody bothers Milt?

"I guess I wouldn't know anything about that," I replied. "But I hear he's pretty thick with Mrs. Bigknife, the widow."

"Between you and me, he visited her before he came in here tonight, but so did a couple of the others. They say she sure does make the best oyster stew. Her reputation among the other people in town is not very good, especially with the womenfolk, from what my old lady says. She also says that Mrs. Bigknife is a likable sort and helps the other ladies in their quilting and such, but they don't treat her very nice in the church meetings, making her sit by herself with the boy when she goes."

Changing the subject, I asked, "Do any Indians ever come in here?"

"You bet. I don't know why they didn't show up tonight, especially ole Flat Paul and his brother, Long Paul. They usually come in before I close up and want some free whiskey or something"

"Do you give it to them?"

"Sure, maybe a shot, and a couple of beers if they clean out the place for me."

"Don't they have money?"

"Heck yes, they got money. They get government handouts every quarter, but it doesn't last long. Ole Flat Paul's squaw only gives him a dollar or two, and he drinks it up fast. Poor ole guy. Long John's not married, but he handles his money better, even farms some further up the foothills on the reservation. Pays somebody to do his irrigating and such." He looked at me like he had just disclosed something important.

"Would that be Mr. Fedderson?"

"Well, yeah, right now Fedderson is doing it, I hear."

"Does he ever come in to your bar?"

"Of course, just about everybody comes in on occasion, even Bishop Thorneycraft comes in once in awhile and drinks a sarsaparilla. They just want to make sure I ain't serving the kids."

"What about Proudmire and the elder Henberry?"

"I just told you, about everybody comes in at one time or another."

"Is Mrs. Cramer around now?"

"Shucks, no! What do you think I am, anyway? She's at the farm house where she's supposed to be, in bed sleeping by now."

"You don't have to get riled up, just curious is all. What does Proudmire drink?"

"Most of the time he'll have a sarsaparilla, especially if he's with the Bishop. When he's alone, he might have a glass of beer. But, if I had to rely on those people for business, I'd be broke."

"Do you go to the church meetings?"

"Not me, but my family is there every Sunday. I got too much work to do catching up around the farm on Sundays, since I have to close this place."

"Well, say, where could a man find a place to sleep around here? I haven't seen any boarding houses or such."

"There ain't no call for such places. When somebody comes to visit, they stay with relatives or close friends, why? You wanting a place to settle for awhile?"

"Not long, just a night or two."

"I have to close up 'til Monday, so I guess you could use my bunk here for a couple o' nights. You can be the night watchman, if you don't mind the accommodations."

As he finished his beer with a big sigh of satisfaction, I drained my glass into my thirsty gullet.

"I was hoping you would make me an offer, even if it is a bit primitive. But, it'll beat sleeping on my horse."

"Grab your poke and make yourself at home, then. There's the stable next door you can put your horse in. I got to get on home."

He grabbed the lamp, and we both exited through the back door. I followed him to the stable where he kept a buggy, and helped him harness the horses. Opening the gate, he rolled out and headed for home. I brought Spottie in, rubbed him down as best I could after removing the saddle, saddlebags, etc., and my bedroll, gave him some hay from the pile at the rear, and returned to Cranky's room with my bedroll and saddlebags, setting the lamp on the table. I went back out and carted my saddle, harness, and horse blankets into the room to make sure that they wouldn't be stolen.

Looking around in the dim light, I noticed the bunk in the corner with a blanket and dirty pillow, a bucket of water sitting on a stool by the small cold stove with the coffee pot on top, and a couple of shelves on the side wall with some cans and a small bag half full of beans or something. I sat down on the same chair and removed my boots, leaving on the rest of my clothes. Putting out the lamp, I felt my way to the bunk, laid down after putting the pillow at the foot of the bed, and in that time between consciousness and slumber was lying there listening to the rustling of the mice or whatever animals were out and about now that it was dark. I was just dozing off, when there was a soft thump on the back door, then some more in rapid succession. It was too high up to be an animal, so I got up and crept to the door, swung it open, and standing there in the dark shadows was Mrs. Bigknife. I held my arm out for her to take and led her into the room. I started to light the lamp, but she said, "Please, please, no light."

I could barely see her in the dark, just the paleness of her face, but I told her to take a seat and asked, "What are you doing out this time of night? It's past midnight. Shouldn't you be home taking care of Charlie?"

"Charlie's all right. He's sleeping soundly now. But that's why I came to see you. I saw you put your horse in there when Cranky left. That old buggy of his makes enough noise to wake up the whole town, especially at this time of night when sounds carry so far." She paused, taking a deep breath, staring at me in the dark. "Earlier, Charlie saw you and Milt Henberry fighting through the dirty window in the bar. He was just coming home from the church, where he had been watching the people dancing, and he said he saw you hit Milt, and Milt crumpled into the bar and onto the floor. Then he heard horses coming, so he rushed home all out of breath and told me what happened. What were you fighting about, Chappie? Is Milt hurt?"

"Nah, he was too drunk to be hurt. His brothers took him home. Why do you care, Mrs. Bigknife?"

"He's a good friend of mine, is all. He comes to see me every time he's in town, and although he's not very handsome, he and Charlie get along pretty good, too. I just don't want to see him hurt."

"Not to worry, Esther. If he gets hurt, it won't be my fault, it'll be his for flying off the handle too readily." He tried to look into her eyes, but her head was tilted downward. She was clasping and unclasping her hands. "There's more to this than just being good friends, isn't there?"

"What do you mean more to it, Mr. Wesford? Milt's just a good friend, one of the few I have around here. The men that come visiting are just acquaintances, even that Mr. Proudmire, and the women tolerate me, but talk behind my back, even when I help with the quilting. Milt's better than that. He likes me."

I watched her in the shadows, looking vulnerable. She was looking at me, and then her features grew darker as she lowered her head, tired looking. Her face was obscured for two or three seconds, then she slowly lifted it and tilted it backward slightly, quickly tossing her hair out of the way. She tried hard to see my face in the dark. My heart started to beat a little more quickly.

"Here, let me get my boots on, and I'll walk you home. We're missing out on a lot of sleep, and whatever's between you and Henberry is none of my business," I told her, but I was going to get to the bottom of it one way or another.

The next morning, I decided to walk to the church meeting since the building was so close. Some people were already gathering, families in wagons, single men and younger boys riding horses, two or three buggies, and everyone dressed up in their Sunday finest. The elder Henberrys went rattling by in a buggy, as if they were late, not saying anything to me as I lumbered along the dirt road kicking at a rock now and then. No sign of the

Henberry brothers, but they would be there sooner or later. I slowed my pace, if that was possible. I wanted to arrive just as the ceremonies were starting, but I wasn't the last one. Widow Bigknife and Charlie were practically running to get there on time. I held the door for them, saying my good mornings, etc., followed them in, and took a seat in the rear by Charlie and Esther, who occupied the last row by themselves on chairs that had been set up in case of an overflow. I figured that this is where they sat every time they attended.

Although I hadn't told anybody that I was a Mormon, I made myself at home as best I could, and sang and prayed along with the others as the meeting progressed. I took a helping of the bread and water as it came around, being passed by a couple of young lads performing their sacramental duties. Two women in the row in front of us turned around and watched as we three took our turns, then they immediately put their heads together and whispered something, giggled, and looked again, giving stern looks of disapproval at Esther. I leaned forward and asked, "Enjoying the show, are you?" Their faces reddened and they turned back around, their husbands shushing at them, whispering to pay attention to the Bishop.

And so the meeting progressed with a short sermon by Mr. Proudmire, an excerpt from the Bible and a lecture by Counselor Carlson on sinful transgressions and the life hereafter, more praying and singing, and an announcement by the Bishop to remind everyone of the upcoming celebrations on the Fourth of July, and finally it was over. Not unlike services down in the valley, I thought, a standard program.

Esther Bigknife and Charlie left quietly during the last hymn. I moseyed outside ahead of the crowd and leaned against the building in the sunshine with one knee bent and my boot heel resting against the wall. Some kids came running out yelling, glad to get out of their restrictions for a few minutes. I saw Jim and Oakley Henberry coming out behind their parents and then the Feddersons and Mrs. Proudmire, none of them talking yet. There may have been a total of 60 or 70 men and women filing out of the church and heading to their wagons and buggies or just walking down the road toward their homes, mothers yelling at their kids, men yelling at their wives to get in the wagon, boys and girls running around every which way laughing and yelling.

Jim and Oakley saw me leaning against the wall and came in my direction all dressed up in suits and vests and polished boots. No one was carrying a gun today out of respect for their religion. I nodded my head in greeting as they approached.

"Mighty fine church service, huh, fellers? That Brother Carlson really gave me something to think about. Yes, sir, mighty fine sermon," I said. "How's that Milt doing this morning, Jim? Not feeling too well?"

"He still has a sore spot on his head where he hit the bar, but he said he's just fine and looking forward to seeing you again. He thinks maybe you had something to do with his condition, ain't that right, Oakley?"

"That's right. He thought maybe you hit him before he took that tumble."

"I'm sorry he feels that way, fellers. Who takes care of all those cows around the cheese factory? I hear your Pa owns them."

"They take care of theirselves. What's your interest in them, anyway?" asked Oakley.

"Mighty fine looking herd, is all. Noticed them yesterday when I was coming into town. Do they give a lot of milk and butterfat?"

"Say, mister, you're mighty curious for a newcomer around here. You got some mischief-making reason or something against them, or maybe thinking about buying Pa out?" Oakley asked.

Jim spoke up, "Ain't never heard anybody ask about butterfat. They usually ask about how much cream. You valley people must be looking to move in up here or something. Is that it? What you nosing around for anyway?"

"Relax fellers. Don't know anyone in the valley who would want to live up here. Gets too cold for good crops, and not enough water, either. Does that Proudmire sell much milk to the cheese factory?"

"Don't know, do we, Oakley? You'll have to ask him. C'mon, we got to get home for dinner."

I went back to Cranky's place and ate a couple pieces of jerky from my saddlebag, pondering my next move. I saddled up Spottie and decided to spend the afternoon taking a ride; it was too nice a day to be cooped up in the back end of a bar. Heading up the road that runs along the creek where the wagon had been pulled out, I continued on to the northwest, following the creek into the mountains above the settlement. I discovered there was a small lake where the stream had been dammed up. The dam was about 50 feet high and had a chute to let out water on one side. Spottie and I took a tour around the area, noticing that one side of the canyon was not fit to be climbing around on because of its steepness. The stream above feeding into the lake was small for draining the water out of the higher elevations, but it didn't look like it ever got a great amount of runoff by the markings on the canyon walls. The lake itself was about half full. With all the snow up there in the wintertime, I would have thought there would have been a lot more water. Going away from the lake into a small canyon, there was a small cabin and stable with a shed, vacant now. I went back by the lake and found a cool spot under the trees and picked some blackberries from the bushes, eating them as I picked. They were big and delicious, and made a fine treat after the jerky. I kept a sharp eye out for any wildlife, especially black bears that might have the same idea.

I ate a few more of the berries then hopped on Spottie for the ride back down to town. About a half-mile below the dam, as the mountains were beginning to peter out a shot rang out, and I slumped over in the saddle like I had been shot, then fell to the ground with Spottie running on. Laying there without noticeably moving, I slowly got my pistol ready for business, and it wasn't long before I heard voices and the noise of horses clomping along.

"There he is over there. Keep him covered while I take a look."

I lay perfectly still as the culprit dismounted and walked a couple of steps to my "dead" carcass, and as he rolled me over, he was staring into the long barrel of my revolver.

"Drop your pistol, Milt, and tell Oakley to drop his, too, unless he wants a dead brother."

"Darn you, Oakley, why didn't you shoot him when I turned him over. Now he's got us covered. You might as well drop your gun and come on over here before he kills us both."

"You fellers been out bear hunting right after church on a Sunday? Don't you know it's a day of rest, and don't you know the difference between me and a bear, huh? What the devil you trying to kill me for?"

Milt gave me an extremely dirty and aggravated look, as Oakley joined him.

"You boys need a little more practice before you go off and shoot at anything in sight."

I gave a whistle and Spottie came trotting up and stopped a yard or two behind me.

"Well, now, turn around, both of you and drop your gun belts before I start getting agitated. ..... Good, good. Now start walking west and don't look back."

They had gone about thirty yards when I told them to halt.

"You gents won't be needing your horses this afternoon," I said as I picked up the reins of Milt's animal and walked over to Oakley's, holding the men in my sights.

"You ain't going to leave us up here with no food or horses, are you?" Oakley asked in a perturbed tone. "Its twenty miles back home."

"Well, I hope you enjoy your hike! It'll be dark in a couple of hours, so you better get to walking! Next time you take a pot shot at me, you better make it a good one. I ain't too fond of that practice, so you better watch out. I saw Milt tailing me way back there, and you, Oakley, when you joined him still in your church clothes. Have a nice walk, gentlemen!"

I could hear Milt yelling at Oakley 'til they were out of sight down the hill. He didn't like their predicament at all. I gave them a few more minutes walking time, and then I retrieved their gun belts and pistols, draped them over the saddle horn of one of their horses, mounted Spottie and returned to town with the animals to Cranky's small stable. Making sure they had enough feed and water, I snatched the Henberry armament from its resting place and went into my temporary accommodations. I dropped them on the table for Cranky to find with a note telling him to return them to the Henberry brothers. By now, the sun was setting and dusk was gathering. I rummaged around and found some coffee grounds and having boiled it on the small stove, sat down at the table, and was enjoying the hot, dark nectar.

But, not for long. I heard someone thumping on the door again just as I was beginning to relax in the flickering lamplight being cast by the contraption I had hung on a nail by the entrance to the bar area. Opening the door, Mrs. Bigknife was standing there. She said, "Mr. Wesford, Chappie, I saw you putting Milt's horse in the stable. Where is he and what are you doing with his horse?"

"Why, he and that Oakley wanted to walk home from the mountains up there by the small lake, so I told them I would take care of their horses for them. They should be about halfway home by now. Not to worry, Mrs. Bigknife. They're just fine, and will pick up their horses tomorrow, I'm sure."

"Walking home? They never walk anywhere if they can help it! What have you done to them?"

"Now, Esther, I ain't done nothing to them. Like I said, they're fine."

"Well, I don't care that much about young Oakley, but if you've hurt Milt, Mr. Henberry's going to be awful mad, and so will I," she said, angrily.

"Let me walk you home again. It's dark already, and I wouldn't want you to stumble and fall and hurt yourself. Where's Charlie?"

"He's eating his supper."

On the way to her place, I reassured her about the Henberrys, and asked her again about her connection to Milt. Why is she being so protective of him? There has to be more than friendship. But, she just brushed me off, and asked, "Would you like to come in and have some roast beef? Charlie and I have plenty to share."

We had a pleasant repast, but I could get no more information out of her. I couldn't believe the rumors that I had heard about her and the men folk. She was too smart for that to happen, but she had something to do with them. What?

CHAPTER 6

Early the next morning I cleared out of Cranky's place in case the Henberrys came looking for me, and watched the sunrise from a knoll south of town sitting under a cedar tree. It was an advantageous spot to observe the comings and goings on the Six-Mile Road. I didn't have to wait long to see the three Henberry brothers traveling at a fast clip heading toward town. When they were out of my sight, I mounted Spottie and headed down Six-Mile Road to have a parley with the elder Henberry.

I found Mr. Henberry in his stable, saddling up a horse.

"Howdy there, Mr. Henberry. Getting ready to take a ride?"

"Howdy to you, too, Mr. Wesford. Yes, I was going to go check on my cows up near the creamery. I heard there was a couple that wasn't well."

"Saw your boys heading to town. I guess they won't get much grain ground today, will they? Any idea what they were going to town for?"

"Nope and nope. They told me they had some unfinished business to attend to. What do you care, anyway?"

"Why have they been following me around, and why would they try to bushwhack me up near the mountains? Any ideas?"

He gave me a steely stare with his partially closed eyes, and then relaxed.

"Nary a one. What do you mean, bushwhack?"

"That Oakley has been taking pot shots at me. He and your boy Milt almost got me yesterday. I'm not too partial to being shot at, Mr. Henberry. You better call them off before somebody gets hurt, and it ain't going to be me."

"I'll have a talk with them, Chappie, but now I got to get on to those sick cows," he said, climbing on his horse.

"Would appreciate your talking to them, yes sir, I would. You can also tell them that I plan to be around here a mite longer looking at things that interest me, and their cooperation would be downright helpful."

He gave a wave of his head and made those giddy-up sounds with his mouth, urging his horse to exit the stable.

I was still astride Spottie on the other side of the fence, and came alongside Henberry as he passed through the gate. "Do you mind if I ride along with you. I'd sort of like to see your herd and the cheese-making factory, if you don't mind. Never had a close look at one."

"Let's go!" he yelled, urging his horse to a run.

We went flying up the road until we reached the area of the hills, then we slowed down to a normal pace and turned off the road through some untouched country for a little ways coming to an old wooden fence with a gate. Henberry dismounted, unlatched the gate and swing it open into the hillside field. I led his horse through, and he closed the gate, remounted, and we continued with neither of us saying anything. Up over the side of the hill, through the cedars and up the side of another hill. We stopped when we reached the crest of the hill, and I had to admire the view of some cows grazing peacefully in the grass in the valley below us. To our right was a long hill slanting gently upward with a few more animals grazing or laying in the sun or under a cedar tree. To the left was a mostly flat, grassy area with a stream running through it, and almost straight ahead a mile or so, I could see the stable and barn area. An ideal setting.

Still not speaking, we trotted to the buildings where Mr. Henberry dismounted and yelled, "Hey, Eddie, come on out here? We got a visitor!"

A short, slight feller came walking across the stable yard, climbed through the fence rails, and said, "Good morning, Jim. Max and I herded those two sick ones into the barn to keep them separate like you ordered. What do you suppose is wrong with them?"

He was glancing back and forth between Henberry and myself as he spoke, trying to size me up.

"This gent here is Chappie Wesford from down in the valley, Eddie Jensen," he introduced the cowhand. "He wanted to take a look at our dairy operation and the creamery, so I brought him along. Are those cows any worse than yesterday?"

"Let's go take a look and you can see for yourself. Maybe this feller will know what's ailing them," Eddie said.

All the animals I'd seen this morning looked fat and healthy up till now. The two sick ones were scrawny and listless, just standing with heads down.

"They been like that for a couple a days, now, Mr. Henberry, and are awful messy with watery movements, like diarrhea," the other gent in the barn, Max, put in. Max was a strapping, blond youth about the same age as Oakley, I thought, but more muscular and a little taller.

"Did you give them some of that tonic for the scours?" asked Jim.

"Not yet. Thought you better look at them first."

"Well, they probably got into some bad hay or eating too much. Give them some of that, and watch them for another day. If they don't start improving, give them a diarrhea ball and another dose of tonic. Try that and see how it goes. If that doesn't work, we'll try something else. Got any ideas, Wesford?"

"Sounds like the scours, all right. I'd do just what you recommended."

"At least, we agree on something. Let's go up to the creamery and see how they're doing."

We were about half-way up the long hill, when we saw the young Henberrys riding down toward us. They had retrieved the two horses from Cranky's stable.

"There he is! What's he doing with our Pa?" Oakley, spotting me first, yelled.

They came racing toward us, their horses' hooves sliding to a halt ten yards up the hill with guns drawn aimed at yours truly.

"What's that coward doing out here, Pa? You being forced to ride along with him?" Milt asked in a loud voice. "I got a hankering to let him have it right now for stealing our horses yesterday and making us walk home."

"Settle down, Milt," the elder Henberry cautioned. "And put your guns away. You boys deserve what you got. There weren't any reasons to go shooting at him first."

"I got plenty of reasons," replied Milt. "In the first place I don't like him, he's an outsider, he's a know-it-all valley conniver, and a rotten, inquisitive inner-, inner, uh-, what's that word, I'm trying to think of, Jim?"

"Interloper?"

"Yah, that's it, interloper! An' he's been making disparaging remarks about some people I know. I owe him a bullet just for that."

"Who might that be?" I asked, knowing full well he meant Mrs. Bigknife.

But he didn't get a chance to answer. I pulled my pistol from its holster and fired at a small flock of sparrows flying by, hitting one, and then another before they disappeared into a cedar tree. It happened so fast and expertly, it startled their horses, causing them to rear up and try to run away.

It took a minute or two for the Henberrys to get their animals under control and get their own startled expressions back to normal.

"Who might that be, Milt?" I asked again, as Spottie stood without moving a muscle. He had been through this so many times before, it didn't bother him.

"Uh...uh..."

"Now, listen here boys!" the elder Henberry began. "I don't want none of you getting hurt over a little gossip.

Chappie and I were just going up to have a look at the creamery. Don't you have some work to do down at the mill? C'mon, Chappie."

I watched as the brothers took off, and then urged Spottie to a trot to catch up with the old man.

"That was some shooting there, knocked them birds right out of the sky. Are you some kind of lawman or something?"

"Just keeping in practice, is all," I replied. "It'd be a shame if I had to shoot one of your sons over such trivial matters, wouldn't it?" Changing directions, I continued, "How much cheese does that factory make in a month? How much milk do you use in the process? Does it all come from your herd? How many cows you got down there, anyway? Who does all that milking? Does Proudmire ever sell you any milk?"

"Now, hold on there, Chappie. You're going to have to ask Calderson those questions. I don't get too involved in the day-to-day stuff. We'll be there in a few minutes, as you can see."

The building looked bigger on the inside than it did from the outside. There were three long metal vats or open tanks about waist high on wooden supports taking up most of the space, the insides having a slight incline to a drain at one end of each. The boiler was near the dock area where the milk containers were dropped off, and long tables lined one side with racks behind. Two men with long handled paddles were working the vats, and another one was down by the boiler.

Henberry introduced me to George Calderson, and then he said he had something to do and left.

Mr. Calderson was a likable sort. I'd seen him in the church meeting, but didn't know that was him. He explained to me the cheese-making process, or at least parts of it, starting with, "Over there, Mr. Wesford, is the milk receiving area. Those cans are all empty now. Monday is a pretty slow day around here, since most of the farmers don't get around to bringing their excess milk in but once a week, usually Wednesday or Thursday. Those fellers there with the long paddles are working the curds that come from the boiler and draining off the whey. You know curds and whey, that's what happens when you mix in some ingredients and heat your milk, curds and whey. The whey runs out of the vats through drainpipes to barrels, which catch it, and the farmers pick it up and feed it to their pigs, those farmers that have pigs. Only a couple of them own enough pigs to spend time getting the whey. Those gents squeeze all the whey out of the curds and put the curds into a press there, by the tables, in small crates or baskets lined with some cloth, packing in as much as they can and squeezing even more whey out of it. That about does the process. It sits there on the shelf for a couple of days, and then is moved to another shelf to age before it's sold to a store. That's about it, all right."

"How much cheese is produced in a month?"

"It depends, yes sir, depends on several factors, the first of which is the volume of milk the farmers bring to us, and there's the butterfat content of the milk. The higher, the better. Then there's the seasonal variation, the number of cows being milked, all that stuff enters into it. You can get about two pounds of cheese from five gallons of milk. So, if fifty farmers bring us a hundred gallons a month, it would give us a ton of cheese. Sometimes it's a little more, but more often than not it's less."

"I guess you pay the farmers something for their milk, don't you. They don't just give it to you, do they?"

"Of course. Mr. Henberry determines the amount. How, I don't know, but he tells me once a month or sometimes more often how much."

"Do you pay some farmers more than others?"

"It's all determined by the fat content. Some farmers just have better cows than others, so there is some variation, yes."

"What about Roger Proudmire? How much milk does he deliver each week, and does he get the same as other farmers?"

He gave me a funny look and said, "As far as I know, it's the butterfat content that determines the price."

"And who determines that?"

"I do, and Mr. Henberry checks all the figures."

"Who buys most of the cheese?"

"A store down in the valley and Mr. Thorneycraft buys some for his store to sell here in town. But there's a buyer comes to town about once every three months from the valley and buys the bigger part of it. All this stuff we're making today will go to him. Say, you being from down there might know him. Name's Bohannon. I ain't never seen him myself. He deals with Henberry at his place, I guess, and sends somebody to pick it up."

"Bohannon, huh? Bohannon, hmm-m, don't reckon I'm familiar with the name." I paused, like I was thinking and asked, "Who are the pig farmers that pick up the whey?"

"It mostly goes to Mr. Proudmire and ole Cranky Cramer. Why?"

"Just wondered. Thanks for the introduction to cheese-making. There's nothing better than a good hunk of cheese on a piece of bread, no sir."

"Any time."

"Say, do you know if Mrs. Bigknife ever buys any cheese?"

"If she did, she'd get it at the store, but I have seen her and Henberry in the office when she picks up some whey for her pigs on occasion."

"Thanks, Mr. Calderson. I'll be going now."

As long as I was in the town proper, I decided I would pay another visit to Esther Bigknife and maybe talk to Proudmire.

"Hi, Charlie. Ready for another ride on Spottie?" I asked the boy dressed in a pair of old overalls and nothing else, who was playing marbles in the dirt by himself outside her house.

"You bet, Mr. Chappie!" He hopped up and came over to rub Spottie's nose.

"We better ask your mother first."

He went running into the house yelling, "Ma! Ma! Can I ride Spottie again, can I, huh? Please, Ma! Chappie, uh, Mr. Wesford, asked me if I wanted to! Please, Ma!"

"Good day, Mr. Wesford," she said, from the doorway, as Charlie came running back out. "How far you going this time with Charlie?"

"We'll go about as far as the creek and back. C'mon, Charlie, let's get you up in the saddle this time! That's it. How does that saddle feel? I'm going to climb on behind now, so hold the reins."

I waved at Mrs. Bigknife who was still standing in the doorway watching us, and told Charlie how to get the horse going. "Just say giddy-up, Spottie. You hold on to those reins with one hand and grab the saddle horn with the other," as Spottie started walking leisurely.

Up to the creek and back. I showed Charlie how to get him to turn around or turn this way and that, and we practiced whoaing and holding on. "Next time, you can go by yourself. How would that be?"

"Goll-ee, that would be fine! Really fine!"

"Well, Mrs. Bigknife, Charlie's going to be a good horseman, aren't you, Charlie? He learns almost as fast as Spottie does," I said and laughed.

"Now, he'll never quit begging me to get him a horse! Thanks a lot, Mr. Wesford!"

"We ain't going on anymore rides if I hear you're pestering your mother about owning a horse, Charlie, so you just play it straight for awhile 'til you're a little older. Got that?"

"All right, Mr. Wesford," he conceded with a thoroughly dejected countenance.

"Come in, Mr. Wesford, I still have some of that beef left, I'll fix you some lunch," she urged.

"Why, thanks, and call me Chappie, please."

I followed her into the kitchen again and sat down at the table. Charlie went back to playing marbles in the dirt.

"It'll just take a minute or two to heat this up. I made some stew this morning out of the leftovers. How about a cup of tea?"

"I'll just drink water, if you have enough in the bucket. Otherwise, I'll get you some to earn my bread."

"No need. There's plenty," she said, dipping the dipper into the water and pouring it into a glass."

"What brings you here today, Chappie? Milt told me this morning what you did to him and Oakley, and he was awful mad, you can bet on that."

"I don't suppose he mentioned that they tried to kill me, did he? Yes, they took a shot at me, and wanted to make sure I was dead. But, I wasn't."

She sat down and looked at me quizzically.

"I don't think they'll try it again after I had a talk with ole man Henberry."

"You better be careful, 'cause they don't always do what their Pa tells them," she warned with a concerned expression, brushing the dark hair away from her face.

Before she turned away, I asked, "How many pigs you got out there penned up?"

"Just two for now. Why?" She got up and went to the cupboard, removing two bowls, then to the stove and dipped out some stew. I had to admire her graceful movements as she placed the bowls on the table, one at a time. "This got awful hot. You might have to wait until it cools off before you can eat it."

"Sure smells good, but only two bowls? Isn't Charlie going to eat anything?"

"This one's for him. I'm just not hungry right now. You go ahead and I'll call Charlie to wash up."

"It just don't seem right, does it Charlie, us eating all this good stew, and your mother just watching it disappear?"

"No, sir, it sure don't. But it sure is good."

"Who feeds them pigs, Esther? You or Proudmire?"

"I do! Why would he have anything to do with them, after he sold them to me? I feed them with the help of Charlie. Don't we Charlie?"

"What kind of feed you give them?"

"Anything I can find, barley, wheat, whey, old stuff we don't eat, vegetable greens and such, and lots of old bread. Why? You sure ask the dumbest questions. You know what pigs eat." She sounded upset that I should ask such a question.

"How do you get the whey from the creamery, and how do you pay for all that stuff?"

"How I pay for it is none of your business, Mr. Wesford. Cranky either helps me with the whey or I borrow his buggy is how I get the whey. I'm going to have to ask you to leave, if you keep up with your stupid questions."

I gave her some time to calm down by watching Charlie as he finished his stew, then he got up and went back outside without a word.

"I didn't mean to upset you, Esther. Just wondered is all. I hear Cranky and Proudmire both have some pigs, too. How many do you suppose they have?"

"I don't know. You'll have to ask them. Why are you asking all these questions?"

Without answering, I asked, "Do you and ole man Henberry have some sort of business deal?"

She looked at me like I was crazy. "I see him once in awhile at the creamery. He's the richest man around here with all those cows and that mill, and the land. He owns a lot of the land around here. So, when I pick up the whey, I usually find out how Mrs. Henberry is doing if he's there. She was awful sick last winter, had the influenza and almost died, poor woman. I don't know what he'd do without her."

"It's been a few months since winter. Is that the only thing you talk to him about?"

She gave me another dirty look. "Well, he never comes to my house, so I don't know how they're doing unless I catch him at the creamery office. Besides, he worries about Milt when he gets drunk, so I let him know what Milt's been up to."

"He sure gets a lot of looking after, don't he, that Milt feller? Looks to me like he's old enough to take care of himself, if he'd lay off the liquor."

"Some people got to go through that, don't they, Chappie, before they hit their stride."

She picked up the dirty bowls and placed them in a wash pan by the pail of water, but didn't make any attempt to clean them.

"It's been nice talking with you, Esther, and thanks for the stew. It was mighty fine tasting. I guess I better be moseying along before you get mad and get your pea shooter off the shelf over there."

She smiled, but didn't say anything as I walked out the door.

CHAPTER 6

The "dirty ole rascal" Fedderson was at home when I knocked on the door, that is, he wasn't in the house, but out in back messing with his chicken coop, his daughter, I assume it was his daughter, said. She was a pretty young thing about 12 years old, I would guess. I hadn't noticed her among all the boys and girls at the dance, but I wasn't paying much attention to the kids.

Walking around the corner of the house, I could hear hammering, bam-bam-bam-bam, and then it stopped. As I got closer to the structure that housed the fowls, it commenced again, bam-bam-bam-bam-bam-bam, in rhythmical percussions. I found Fedderson pounding on the boards on the back wall of the coop. It was a ramshackle edifice made out of old barn wood pieces thrown together with a vengeance. The pounding stopped and the chickens quit cackling at the disturbance when I said, "Doing a little repair work there, Mr. Fedderson? Sounds like you're pretty busy."

"Afternoon to you! Yes, I had to nail a board back to the wall. A badger or a weasel got into the coop last night and stole a chicken or two, so I'm fixing it so they can't get in, I hope. What brings you by?"

"Not much. Was just over visiting with the widow and her son, and thought maybe I'd stop by and say hello. Your daughter told me you were out here messing with the chicken coop. Nice girl. I take it she's the youngest one of the family?"

"She's our baby, all right. Darlena is her name, if she didn't tell you. There's her and Hilaine, and my two boys, Freddy and Max. Freddy and Max ain't home much. They both got jobs right now."

"I hear that youngest Henberry boy's been flirting a lot with Hilaine, is it? I saw them dancing together quite a few dances the other night."

"He's quite smitten by her for sure, but my wife keeps her eye on them."

"Does that Max work for Henberry?"

"How did you know that?" Not giving me time to answer, he continued. "He's working there for the summer, milking and herding cows. Freddy is working for ole Cranky Cramer, feeding pigs, and such. He's trying to save up money to go on a trip back east on that train. He's got itchy feet. Now, Max, he's just the opposite, wants to stay around here, get married, and own a farm someday. I expect they'll find a place of their own before too long."

"How many pigs does Cramer have?"

"Probably around a hundred, Freddy says. I ain't never been there, where the pig farm is. It's further away from town, maybe another five miles, according to Freddy, northeast in the basin near where the Shroud River comes out of the mountains. It's right on the edge of the Ute Reservation over there, if you want to take a look. Just follow the road that goes north a couple miles east of here."

"I guess Freddy picks up the whey from the creamery then for the pigs, huh?"

"Yah. He usually stops by home for lunch when he makes the trip. I tell him he's got to get another job; the pig smell is all over him. Hahaha!" he laughed. "But he tells me it's the smell of money he smells."

"I guess the Proudmires live on that road, too?"

"Yah. There place is on the road to the east. Just don't take that road north. If you do, you end up at Cramer's."

"Did you ever hear of the widow associating, for the lack of a better word, with the older Henberry?"

He gave me a funny look, like I had overstepped my bounds.

"Nah. That Milt's the only one hangs around there, as far as I know from the gossip. Why?"

"You never seen them together, huh?"

"Nope. Even though I live here in town, I don't know everything that goes on. Big Jim visits Cramer's establishment once in a while, and so do I for that matter, but I ain't never seen the widow in there."

It was getting late in the afternoon, so I told him, "Nice talking to you, Cal. I'll be going on my way."

"Why don't you stay for supper? Barbara always cooks up plenty, 'cause she never knows who'll be stopping by."

"Hm-m. Well, I ain't too hungry. I had dinner with the widow about an hour ago. But, I'll stay, if you think your wife won't care."

"Good! Settled! She won't mind a bit, and she always says she'd rather feed two hungry men than one that isn't hungry, 'cause they always eat less. We still have some daylight left, why don't you grab a hoe and help me do a little weeding. My garden's getting overrun."

"You're going to make me work for my porridge, huh? Where's a hoe?"

The two men went to work. Chappie was cutting and throwing weeds right and left as if he enjoyed the labor, and didn't say much, hoping he could keep up with the feller on the next row, who had a lot more experience. The sun was beginning to set over the western mountain range when Fedderson said, "Let's go eat. We about finished the whole garden. Barbara will be surprised."

"I ain't done this in a few years, but it all came back once I got into the swing of it. I think I've earned a pound of potatoes and a huge steak, but I'll settle for whatever's there!"

They washed up and went into the house that was filled with the aromas of cooking.

"I asked Chappie to eat with us, Barb. We got another plate, don't we?"

"He can use yours," she joked. "Darlena, set another plate on the table for Mr. Wesford. Make yourself at home, Mr. Wesford, right there at the table."

The meal was consumed with eagerness and very little talk. As Chappie pushed his empty plate back from the edge of the table, smacked his lips, and began to say how much he had enjoyed the fixings, a knock was heard at the front door.

Hilaine jumped up almost knocking her chair over, and rushed to the door, saying, "I'll see who it is, Mother!"

The family knew who it was without even looking, as Hilaine said, "C'mon in, Oakley. You're a little bit early tonight. And you too, Ned, come in. Are you fellows hungry?"

They both took off their hats and Oakley responded, "No, but thanks." Seeing Chappie at the table, continued, "Looks like we came at a bad time, but it was our turn to do the ward teaching again," still staring at Chappie. "We can come back later, or maybe tomorrow night."

"Come on in, Ned and Oakley," Mr. Fedderson said. "We just have a dinner guest, and I don't imagine Chappie would mind hearing the teachings tonight, would you Chappie?"

"Not at all, except I haven't met that fellow with Oakley. Did you say his name was Ned?"

"Unh-huh. This is Ned Carlson, Chappie Wesford," replied Cal. "Ned is an Elder, just returned from a mission and the son of Counselor Carlson that spoke in church yesterday."

"Oh, yes. Nice to meet you, Ned," Chappie said and shook Ned's hand.

"If you're all done eating, why don't we go into the front room, where there's more space," Mrs. Fedderson suggested. "Darlena and I will gather up the dishes and be in there before you know it."

In the front room, I found a seat on the piano bench, Hilaine sat on the settee next to Oakley's chair, and Cal sat in his easy chair after he finished moving chairs from the kitchen for Ned and Oakley.

Since the teachers weren't making any attempt to start their prayer and teaching, I asked Oakley, who was only paying attention to Hilaine, "Well, Oakley, been doing any hiking or shooting lately?"

He looked at me with eyes that could have thrown daggers if it were possible, but said, "Not too much, Mr. Wesford. Me and Milt went hiking for awhile yesterday afternoon to do some hunting for a polecat that's been roaming around. Just got off one shot at it, though, before he got lost in the brush. Sure would've liked to have his carcass to mount on the wall."

Mr. Fedderson and Hilaine didn't know that we were talking about our little scrape, but were listening and watching to learn more.

"A polecat would sure make a good trophy, all right, but they're awfully smart and cagey. By the way, aren't you a little old to be doing this teaching? I would think the Elder would bring along a younger person to help him out and to learn the whys and wherefores of it."

Oakley started to squirm and turn red, looked at Hilaine and back at me. "The Bishop asked me to fill in 'cause all the younger boys are too busy during the summer." He looked at Mr. Fedderson and hoped he would step in and help out, but Cal got up and left the room.

I said, "Another thing, down in the valley, when I was doing it, the church always made sure that they had asked a person of good moral upbringing and integrity to help out. Some of the younger men are not always what they profess, but I'm sure you're not in that category, are you?"

He was going to reply, but Darlena and her mother and father came into the room, Darlena sitting by Hilaine on the settee, and her mother in the other easy chair.

Ned had been listening closely to our conversation, but kept quiet.

"Well, Ned, we're all here," Cal advised. "You and Oakley can get started on your sermon for today, right Barbara?"

"I hope it's not a long one," she replied. "We still have the dishes to wash and dry."

"I'm sure it will be short 'cause Oakley is more interested in courting our beautiful daughter than trying to teach us old folks anything," said, Cal, and laughed.

Ned smiled, too, as Oakley turned red. Ned began, "I would like to start this evening with a prayer. You can all please join in, if you know it."

After the prayer, he continued, "Our lesson tonight is on Why it is Important to Lead a Good and Moral Life. Oakley, would you begin by explaining what a good and moral life means in the teaching of the Latter Day Saints?"

"Before Oakley gets started," I said, "I'd like to ask him, does he believe that men who kill, or just attempt to kill another person, fits in to that description of a good and moral life?"

Oakley looked at me with a sour expression, but began, "It depends...depends on the...," but he was interrupted by a loud knocking on the front door.

"Just a minute!" yelled Cal, getting up to see who was there.

Standing at the door was Widow Bigknife looking very excited. "Is Oakley in there? Tell him to get over to the saloon quick! Milt is tearing up the place! I don't know what he's doing but Charlie said he saw him through the window throwing chairs, cussing, and...and..."

Oakley went running out the door almost knocking Fedderson and Esther down, and jumped on his horse before she could finish, and raced down the road toward the tavern.

I spoke up, "I think I'll go see what Milt's doing. I heard he gets wild when he drinks too much. Thanks for dinner!" I told the Feddersons, as I climbed on Spottie.

"Tell Oakley to be careful!" yelled Hilaine.

By the time I reached Cranky's, everything was calm and peaceful. Cranky was telling Oakley, "I'm sorry I had to do it, but he lost his head and was going berserk in here, breaking my furniture, throwing glasses, chasing out my customers. What's the matter with him?"

"I don't know, Cranky. Sometimes he gets like this for no reason," Oakley replied. "I'll take him home and let him sleep it off. Can you give me a hand with him?"

"I'll give you a hand, Oakley," I said. "Where is he?"

He looked at me and said, "He wouldn't want you touching him, after what you already done to him. Cranky can help me."

"I ain't going to help him," stated Cranky, "and I'm not going to let him in here anymore, either. You can tell him that he's barred from my place 'til he learns how to behave himself, and he owes me some money for all the damage he did. I drug him back behind the bar here, to get him out of sight."

Widow Bigknife came in out of breath and looked directly at me, "What did you do to him this time? Where is he? Is he hurt?"

I just returned her gaze and shrugged my shoulders.

"Now, now, Esther," Cranky said. "He didn't do anything to Milt. I had to give him a little tap on the head to stop him from destroying the place. He's back here lying on the floor, still out."

Oakley went behind the bar to attend to the unconscious Milt. Chappie and Esther followed along. It was getting crowded in the small space between the bar and the back wall with all four of them in there.

"C'mon, Oakley, let's get him loaded up," Chappie suggested. "I'll take him by the legs, and if you get him under the shoulders, we'll have him on his horse in no time."

Oakley reluctantly relented, as Esther stood staring.

"Good riddance," offered Cranky.

Before we could get him on the horse, Esther had to take his face in both hands and plead, "Milt, Milt, darling! Wake up, wake up! You're going to be all right! Wake up!"

There must have been a subconscious reaction to her touch or sound, because he let out a long slow moan, "Unnh-nn-o-nn-n," but he didn't wake up.

We hoisted him onto the horse, and went back into the tavern. Oakley walked up to the bar facing Cranky and said, "I'll ask Pa to come by and pay you something for the damages, but I don't know whether I should thank you or not. You must've hit him pretty hard to put him out for that long."

"I think he was about ready to pass out anyway. I just hastened it up a bit. He was drunker than usual, if that's possible. His Pa ought to do something about his drinking."

"Nobody can do anything about that, Cranky," Esther said. "It's just the way he is and always will be. I'm sorry for thinking you did it, Chappie, but I thought..."

"That's all right, Esther. Glad to be of help for a change....to you too, Oakley," I replied.

"I better get him home," Oakley said, and walked out the door.

I looked around the tavern. "There's a chair still upright at that table there, Esther. Care to have a sarsaparilla before you go home, that is, if Cranky has any unbroken glasses?"

She glanced at the preoccupied barkeep, and then looked into my eyes. "I'd like that, Chappie. Set them up, Cranky, and have a drink with us."

"By crimany, I think I will," he said, grabbing three glasses from under the bar and a quart bottle of sarsaparilla. "Let's all drink to Milt Henberry, the rage of Altveel," he said, sitting down at the table and pouring the glasses full.

There were noises from outside and the door burst open to let in two of the young local cowboys. "Give us something to drink, Cranky!" one yelled. "We're awful thirsty from milking all those cows of Henberry's!"

Cranky didn't get up from his chair, but said, "Set that table up there, boys, and have a seat! I'll be right with you. What you drinking tonight?"

They ignored his suggestion, stopped as they reached the bar, and looked around. "By golly, Cranky, it looks like a hurricane's been through here. Was Milt on one of his rampages again?"

Cranky arose from his seat and walked behind the bar, "Let's just say, he was a might upset about something," and looked over at me. "You know how he is. What will it be, Mike? A beer or something stronger, if I can find a glass?"

"I'm having beer out of that keg there. What you want, Wonder?"

"I was just wondering about that, if you was going to drink beer or something else. I wonder how a sarsaparilla would taste, Cranky, since that is all I can afford," the one called Wonder replied.

Cranky reached beneath the bar and brought up two glasses then filled them both with beer, saying, "I'll furnish you fellers a beer or two, if you help set this place to rights. That beer keg is about the only thing still standing, plus a few quart bottles down below. How about it?"

"That's the best deal I've heard in a long time, and I was wondering when you were going to ask," Wonder said. "C'mon Mike. You set up the tables and chairs and stuff, and I'll grab a broom and help get all the broken glass."

"Soon as I drink this beer," said Mike. He looked around the room at the disorderly mess, and settled his sights on the only female around. "Out for a night on the town, Widow Bigknife? Who's the feller sitting there with you? Is he looking for some oyster soup this evening?"

"Now, don't go starting no trouble, Mike," Cranky cautioned. "That feller is from out of town, minding his own business, and it ain't none of yours to be bothering him."

Esther spoke up, "Drink your beer, Mike, and leave us alone. This gentleman is a friend of mine," with the emphasis on "gentleman."

"Whoeee! A gentleman now is it you'd be keeping company with, huh, Widow? Ain't the men around here good enough for you anymore? You got to be seeing a gentleman, now, huh? Whooeee! Did you hear that, Wonder?"

"I was wondering who he was," replied Wonder. "I wonder if he really is a gentleman or just an imitation."

Chappie sat through all the palaver, not saying a word. He finished his sarsaparilla, looked at Esther, then looked at the two men standing at the bar doing all the talking. After a long pause, he looked at Cranky then at the two men and said, "Cranky, maybe the teat squeezers at the bar would like to see if they can break some more furniture or something, for that free beer. As a gentleman, I will defend this lady's honor and the insults directed at us, if they would care to indulge."

The one called Mike was waiting for the invitation and stepped forward with an angry countenance, fists clenched, saying, "Come on, Wonder, let's get him," as Chappie rose from his seat.

Mike threw a thunderous right hand that would have put a terrible bruise on the side of anyone's head if it had connected, but Chappie was ready for such a move and ducked under it, stepping forward with a right of his own smack into the solar plexus of Mike, who released a loud gasp and doubled over just to catch another punch under the chin in the throat that partially straightened him back up. Then Chappie threw one more punch that caught Mike by the cheekbone and knocked him down.

Wonder had advanced to a position behind Mike and was getting ready to step up and throw a punch or two when Mike went down. Instead of throwing punches he said, "Hold on there, mister...I was just wondering what happened to Mike. It happened so fast, I didn't get a chance to see it."

"Step up, and I'll give you a demonstration so you don't have to wonder any longer, that is, if you would care to carry on for that feller."

"I don't think that there will be any need for that, no sir, I think I've seen enough. Mike is the toughest feller I ever knew, and he just crumpled right up. I wonder if he knew what hit him."

Cranky spoke up finally, "Why don't you finish your beer and help him up, then clear on out of here. I've got enough broken furniture and stuff."

"That's a good idea, Cranky," replied Wonder. "I'm just going to drink my beer, and then I'll help Mike out to his horse." Long pause. "I was wondering, if Mike doesn't come around, if I could have another beer to drink to this feller's slick fighting? That was some doing, all right. Never seen anything like it."

"I'll buy him another beer, Cranky," said Chappie, "then I'll help him get this gent out of here. Wouldn't want them to leave unhappy."

Before Wonder could finish the beer, Mike let out a moan, shook his head, sat up, rubbed his jaw, and said, "What happened?"

Nobody said anything. All four were watching Mike as he slowly dragged himself up to a standing position. "What happened?" he asked again.

Cranky was the first one to respond. "Have a seat here at the bar, Mike, and finish your beer. Might help you to clear your head. That was a terrible fall you just had, wasn't it, Wonder? I think you better get home and lie down awhile, and have Doc Wetmore take a look at your head tomorrow, if you're not feeling better."

Esther spoke next, "That's a great idea, Mike! You hit your head on a chair seat when you fell," she lied. "How's your eyesight? Can you see things clear? You better get some rest. Wonder here said he would help you get on your horse. Ain't that right, Wonder?"

"You bet! I was just wondering how I was going to do that, if you didn't wake up, then that gent there bought me another beer. But, I'm ready to help you out now."

Mike turned and looked at the generous gent, and it all came back to him, that is, the part of it where he was going to teach the gent a lesson. But the rest of it, he didn't recall. He said, "We'll pick this up where we left off in a day or two, mister, and..."

The door opened in the middle of his sentence, and in walked the elder Jim Henberry.

Cranky started to speak, "Howdy, Mr. Henberry, what....."

But he didn't get a chance to finish, as Henberry asked, "What's been going on here tonight, Cranky? I ran into Oakley and Milt on the way in, and Oakley told me that Milt tore up the place. So I came by to settle up for Milt." Henberry posted his gaze on his two cowhands. "What are you two doing here, Mike? Did you and Wonder have anything to do with this mess?"

Before either one could answer, Chappie put his two cents in. "They didn't have anything to do with it, Mr. Henberry. They just came in a few minutes ago to have a beer after milking your cows. I'm afraid it's all Milt's fault, huh, Cranky?"

"Yup, that's right. Milt got on one of his rampages again and pretty well wrecked the place." Changing the subject, he asked, "Drinking anything tonight, Jim? Mike and Wonder were just finishing up. Ain't that right, boys?"

The two milkmen finished their beers and left without any more trouble.

"You want your usual, Jim?" asked Cranky again.

"Nah. I came into town to talk to Calderson. How much you think I owe you for Milt's damages this time."

Cranky looked around the saloon surveying his furniture. "How about ten dollars? That ought to cover it. He didn't break everything in sight this time."

"I'll just take your word for it, Cranky. Here's the money. I'll be seeing you gentlemen and Mrs. Bigknife. Goodnight."

CHAPTER 7

"Well, he wasn't too friendly, was he?" Chappie asked.

"He's mad at Milt, and came to town to see Mr. Calderson, so it probably ruined his night, too, having to pay out ten dollars to Cranky again," said Esther. "I better get home, too. Charlie'll be wondering where I am."

"I'll escort you home. It's getting pretty late to be walking around alone in the dark," Chappie offered.

"That won't be necessary, Chappie. I only live a hop, skip and a jump up the road."

Cranky was behind the bar since the two milkmen came in, and was there now not paying any attention to the other two customers. He was re-arranging his bottles and glasses, the ones found unbroken on the floor.

"We're leaving, Cranky," said Chappie, getting up from his seat. "But, I'll be back in a few minutes and help you with the clean up."

They left through the rear entrance. On the road they talked about Mike and Wonder, and Esther apologized again for thinking that he had been the one to cause Milt to be unconscious. He had her by the arm, thinking that was the gentlemanly thing to do, but he released his hold and reached down and took her small hand in his. There was no objection. Her hand had a coolness to it, even though the night had not yet turned cold.

He began to tell her about the valley, not mentioning his livelihood, but got on the subject of his fiddle-playing brother and how Ted got carried away with the music, running away from home and learning to play various instruments at some school in New York before the family came west. He said his brother was still married to the woman he met in school, and they had five kids, all musically inclined. And before they knew it, they were at the front door of Esther's house. Charlie must have gone to bed, because there was no light shining through any of the windows, but Esther said he was probably watching for her from the window in the dark. Chappie made sure she had opened her door and then he told her good night. She gave his hand an extra squeeze before saying good night, looking into his eyes as best she could in the small amount of moonlight shining from the east through drifting clouds.

When Chappie returned to the saloon, he found the barkeep setting up the chairs and tables, moving everything to one side.

"Grab that broom there in the corner, and you can start sweeping up the glass," said Cranky.

We had just got started when the front door opened and in popped the two Utes, Long Paul and Flat Paul. Flat Paul saw Chappie sweeping the glass into a pile and went and grabbed the broom.

"My job. You sit."

There was no argument from Chappie, and Long Paul didn't get any argument from Cranky either, when he started setting up tables. Cranky went behind the bar and drew four glasses of beer from the keg, passing one to Chappie, setting two aside for the Utes, and one for himself.

Chappie observed the two Indians working away, then asked, "Which one of you is Long Paul?"

Long Paul stared at him for a full minute before he spoke. "Him, Long Paul," he said, pointing to his brother.

Cranky looked as serious as ever and didn't say a word. Flat Paul hadn't been listening, as he swept away, intent on getting done in a hurry to drink that beer waiting for him.

"Hey! Long Paul!" Chappie raised his voice to make sure the man could hear. "Can I talk to you a minute."

Flat Paul looked up to see who was yelling, looked at Long Paul, who was already drinking his beer, then back to Chappie, who was intently watching him.

"Him deaf injun. That one, Long Paul."

Long Paul broke into loud laughter, "Ha, ha-ha, ha-ha, ha! Preety good joke, no? Ha-ha-ha!"

Cranky began laughing, too, at their little tomfoolery. "Pretty funny, huh, Chappie? Them Utes are funny," still grinning, as he lifted his beer glass.

"Ha-ha-ha! Petty funny all right," Chappie agreed. "Tell me, Long Paul, how long has that Fedderson worked in your fields?"

Long Paul had gone back to setting the place to rights, but he looked around at Chappie, then Cranky, then back to Chappie. "That Fedders' fella plenty good worka', you bet, him do waterin' my hay 'bout three moons now, you bet, good white man. No mind work for Injun Long Paul. He no mind."

"Did he work for you last year?"

"I go his house yesterdee, pay him good money, you bet, no troubles with him. First time I pay him. No work very long. You bet."

Cranky said, "Shucks, you could've asked me that."

Long Paul eyed Chappie to see if he had any more questions, then went back to doing what he had been doing when there were none forthcoming.

"Just wondered," said Chappie.

"It's getting late, and I ain't getting any business, so I'm closing up as soon as these guys are finished. Where you staying?"

"Don't know. Haven't decided that far ahead yet, why?"

"Well, you could stay here in the bar, if you think you could find a spot to throw your bedding. That is, if this is good enough for you?"

"What's wrong with that old two-story building there on the corner, next to where that old man lives? Does he own it? Is he the only one in there?"

"That's old man Weaver's. He lives by himself there in that old house next to it. That old building used to be a hotel. It was always busy with the gold hunters and cattlemen, when it first opened up, I heard. But, when that fizzled, it pretty much fell into disuse. I wouldn't go in there, myself. It's about ready to fall down. I got a bet with old man Henberry that this is the year it's going to crash.

"Ole man Weaver is a cantankerous ole fussbudget, gives everybody a hard time, and just lives on what he saved up. I should say exists. He doesn't live, just exists. Esther looks in on him now and then to see if he's still alive. She says the place is a mess in there. Most everybody's forgotten about him, even the church. He took a shot at the last elder to visit him, so they haven't been there any more. Sometimes he doesn't come out of there for a week or two except his trips to the outhouse. A real odd feller, if you ask me. He hasn't done a thing to that ole hotel since he emptied it out, sold all the furniture and fixings. That was all going on when I showed up in this area about 20 years ago, now. He must be in his eighties, ole fool, but still getting around to do for himself. Goes to Thorneycraft's store just enough to keep himself in fixings, usually on Wednesdays is when I see him hobbling along with his cane and pulling a little wagon to carry his stuff in. Tried to talk to him a couple a times, but he was too busy talking to himself to answer. A strange ole man all right."

Chappie sat through this extended oration without saying a word, just waiting for him to finish. Cranky looked at him over the glass of beer to see his reaction, then Chappie spoke up, "Doesn't he have any relatives? Nobody from out of town ever comes to see him?"

"I heard tell he had a brother came to visit him one time about something or other and they got into a terrible argument. The brother left town and has never come back. I sure would like to know what they were arguing over. Esther said she heard a shot before the brother left. But she didn't know anything more about it. I guess whoever was shooting didn't hit what he was aiming at, but who knows."

"Maybe that's why he chooses to live alone?"

"I don't lose any sleep over it. Ain't none of my business."

Their conversation continued for another few minutes, and by the time they had said everything there was to say about the old man, Long Paul and his brother had finished straightening up the place, and were standing at the bar listening.

"You fellers want another beer?" Cranky asked, already knowing the answer. "One more free, then got to close up."

They each took a big swallow, then Long Paul said, "That ole white man, Weaver, him good friend of Utes, you bet. Him used have Ute wife long time ago. Very happy, laugh all the time, have good time."

He was about ready to say something else, but Flat Paul began, "Ole man Weaver good man. Help Utes many times before white men come. He marry big Chief's daughter, Little Blue Wing. Very happy."

"Even I didn't know that," Cranky said. "Imagine that, married a squaw."

"Wife die, ole man leave Ute country," Long Paul added. "Come back in few years, build those houses where he live. Then him go crazy. No talk to no one no more. Hate everyone. He say him live with wife's ghost."

"That's what he say," Flat Paul chimed in.

"What do you fellers think? You see a ghost over there?" asked Chappie.

They both looked at Chappie with their dark countenances, showing very serious expressions, eyes in a squint.

"Huh-uh, no see ghost," Long Paul answered, "but that ole man do. All the time talking, him say, 'Come Blue Wing, make me dinner, clean house, wash clothes, take off boots,' him say. Then, he do it. No ghost. Crazy in mind, sick."

"When's the last time you talked to him, Long Paul?" asked Cranky.

"Tonight. We stop say hello. He think we are Chief and friend. We leave him alone. Him die soon." Changing the subject, he asked, "You want we clean place tomorrow night?"

"Not tomorrow. You're drinking up all my profits. Next week. Come back next week."

With a look of disappointment, Long Paul said, "Next week, we come back five-six sleeps. Next time we drink whiskey, you bet."

Chappie was getting to know Cranky better, and he decided that he wasn't as cantankerous as he had heard people say. After the Utes left, Chappie asked him, "Anybody around here ever have any trouble with them Utes?"

"None I know of, except the Henberrys. Henberry wanted to build that dam up there on the creek in Little Mouth Canyon, and the Utes were against it, of course, saying it would deprive them of their water downstream. But, they started on the dam anyway, so the Utes attacked them before it was very far along. Killed some animals and set a couple wagons on fire before they could be chased off. There was a big pow-wow with

Henberry, some church officials, and the Utes, and they were able to convince the Utes that it wouldn't interfere with the stream that much, and they had to guarantee them that they would have plenty of water. Well, they all knew that creek goes practically dry every year anyway, especially if we don't get much rain, and when the church fellers threatened to call in the Army on the Utes, they calmed down. So Henberry built the dam, and all has been peaceful since. The Army was already in Utah, so it sounded like a credible threat to the Utes. And there hasn't been any more trouble that I've heard."

"Little Mouth Canyon, huh? I wondered what the name of it was. Who owns that dam now? The Henberrys?"

"I don't think anybody owns it, even though they built it. They just wanted to divert that creek so they could get more water over there near the mill, so they split all the water coming out after they got the dam built. I guess the Utes are getting enough of it. They're not going on the warpath that I heard. They say that the dam is on their land, anyway."

"Do you and Proudmire get enough of it down that way for your pigs and such?"

"We don't need much of that water. We get most of ours from the Shroud River over there to the east, but we had to dig a pretty good ditch to get it to us. I'm surprised the Utes haven't said anything about that."

"Maybe they will. It just takes one bad year of no rain and less snow, and they'll be on the warpath."

"Well, we might have to give it up all together if that happens. The pig market hasn't been very good anyway, at least not up here."

Nothing was said for a minute or two. Both men were thinking of the pork situation, at least Cranky was. Cranky peered at the man sitting at the table nearest to the beer keg from his spot behind the bar wondering why he would be asking questions about the water and the pigs. "What's he doing up here anyway? Who is he? What's he care about the pork market, or is he just making talk?" he thought. "Is he representing some millionaire back east who wants to buy up all the land or what?"

Chappie interrupted the barkeep's thoughts by saying, "I'm going to put my horse in your stable and bring in my bedroll. I think I'll like it here just fine for tonight. Here's a quarter for the beer I drank."

In the morning, Chappie saddled up and left town on the road to the east after he and Cranky had coffee, bacon and biscuits that the bar owner managed to whip together on his small stove. He had decided to take a look at the Proudmire pig farm.

Traveling along the road out of town, he was in no hurry, figuring maybe he could arrive there about noontime and maybe get an invite for a free meal to supplement his foodstuffs (beef jerky and hardtack) that were getting low.

There were some big, fluffy clouds in the sky floating over the mountains from the northwest in a southeasterly direction, almost low enough to reach out and stuff them into a saddle bag, he thought. They didn't look like rainclouds, and even if they became threatening; they usually avoided this area for some unknown reason. But when the rain, came, it could be in torrential amounts, like the one two or three weeks ago that filled the creeks and rivers from bank to bank, even overflowing and extending the waterway outwards in a couple of places.

And Chappie was thinking that his excursion up here was similar to the weather this time of year. He had seen some of the storm clouds already swirl around him, and he hoped they wouldn't develop into a full-grown downpour. He didn't come here for that, but people sure had funny ideas. Some of them just assumed that a stranger in town for awhile had to be up to no good. It wasn't like he wasn't used to seeing this reaction and dealing with some bad hombres. His work as a U. S. Marshal required him to round up all kinds of ne'er-do-wells, to put it mildly. But, why did the General ask him to complete this assignment? It had nothing to do with rounding up the bad hombres, at least as far as he knew, it didn't. He had even left his badge in the valley and brought along his old Union Army uniform to wear at the ceremony day after tomorrow.

He went over in his mind the speech he was going to make as an introduction to the ceremony, something like this, "I was a member of the 2nd Brigade, 280th Pennsylvania Infantry, 10th company, the leader of that company, and I remember the Battle of Gettysburg well. We were in most of the action around Cemetery Hill where some of the most intense fighting occurred, and I was lucky to escape the fate of some of our bravest and most courageous soldiers, who, unfortunately, never left the battlefield alive. I find a very coincidental and refreshing circumstance that I should be selected to be presenting awards to two of my fellow Mormons who both happened to be in the 280th in different companies, and none of us ever knew each other. A very coincidental circumstance and two of them were married to sisters and had never met each other until settling in the hills of Utah Territory. Of course, each knew about the other from their wives' prattle about family affairs in the letters between them. Very odd, all right, but humorous, at least to me, that they are now living in the same town and having a little dispute among themselves. I wonder what their reactions will be when they find out that they had participated together at Gettysburg and both served the country with distinction."

And then, I'll ask them to present themselves front and center and give them their awards, he thought. That won't sound too bad; it's short and to the point and not long enough to create boredom.

But, he still had a couple of days to get through. Things with the Henberrys and friends are reaching the point of getting out of hand, especially with Milt and probably Oakley. That Milt is sure protective or jealous of the Widow. I wonder what the real connection is there. She sure is an attractive woman, even if the rumors are not too nice about her. If I get back to town early enough, I'll have another talk with her. Maybe I can glean some more information out of her. She's about my age, maybe a little younger, and that Charlie is a good looking lad. I'm getting drawn to them over my better judgment. I think I'm getting to like her real well.

She reminds me of my former wife, has that natural air about her as she moves around, and dark hair. Sheila's hair was dark brown, though, but just as long. When we got married, she had short hair, but never cut it afterward. Sadly, she got caught in some crossfire up there in Wyoming when I was hunting that Crawford feller. I'll never forgive myself for taking her to Laramie with me, but she insisted. "I can help you, Chappie, if you take me along," she said. So, I gave in, and now, she's buried there. I ain't seen another woman like her until this Esther Bigknife.

The countryside had been changing, but nothing really startling. He took a look around, noticing the road was dropping in elevation as Spottie trotted his way over the bumps and old dried-up mud holes. There was a beautiful valley opening up to his gaze ahead, looking serene and promising. He could see no movement as he surveyed the scene. There were a few cedar trees scattered around on the bottom, and growing thicker as they crept up the hills in the far distance. He imagined there could be a mountain lion or two roaming the hills, but it wouldn't expose itself by going down into the valley in the daytime. And some black bears around, too, along with all the other animals that claimed this area as home, squirrels, chipmunks, skunks, snakes, prairie dogs on the valley floor, badgers, raccoons, eagles, hawks, all kinds of high elevation birds, a lot of magpies, and all the other smaller animals. He could see dry washes, dry now for the most part, crossing the lower elevations where the water rushed out of the hills and dug a path into the lower depths. A line of trees was growing along where he supposed the Shroud River to be flowing. There were more hills to the south, but the river probably went between them over there to the east. He couldn't make out a distinct opening from his position on the road, but there had to be one because there was no lake that he had heard of over this way. The valley itself looked like the bottom of a drained lake.

He urged the horse to a fast trot, and soon they came in sight and smell of the pig farm. It was just a few acres that had been fenced off, with some feeding troughs along one side of the area and three long pig pens with open fronts on the south side on some high ground. He dismounted by the pens and tied Spottie's reins to the top rail of the wooden fence. He was going to climb over the fence when a young man came out of one of the pens down the line and saw him.

"Hold on, there, cowboy! Where do you think you're going?" he yelled.

"Howdy, there, I was just going' to see what kind of porkers you got here!" Chappie responded. "I hear Mr. Proudmire has a nice crop of them," lowering his voice as the young man came closer.

"Do you have some business with Mr. Proudmire, or are you just looking to grab yourself one and drag him into the woods and cut him up?"

"You look like one of the Feddersons, but I thought that boy worked for the Cramers. What's your name?"

"That's right, mister. I'm Freddy Fedderson. What's it to you?"

"Ah ha. Nothing really, but I've met your other family members, and nice people they are. What you doing here at the Proudmire place, if you don't mind me asking?"

"Ain't none of your business, but Aunt Bessie asked me to come and help out here 'til Brigham gets better. He broke his leg last week. Who are you?"

"I guess you been stuck here and haven't been in to visit your Pa the last few days, and haven't heard all the rumors flying around town?"

"What rumors? Nothing about my family, I hope."

"Oh, no, no. Just rumors about some cowboy snooping around town is all. That would be me, Chappie Wesford, by name. Yup, I been looking around town at things that perk up an interest in me, but haven't been bothering anybody like they say. Are Mr. and Mrs. Proudmire at home now? I'm hoping they'll invite me to dinner. Have you eaten yet?"

Freddy was about 16 years old, blond, muscular, and not used to seeing strangers nosing around the pig pens. He didn't exactly know how to take this fellow. Was he trying to steal a pig, or was he just looking around like he said. It was time for lunch, so he decided to take him to the house and see what happens.

"I was just going to go eat when I saw you looking around. The house is about a half-mile from here to the north, sitting there by the hillside," Freddy said, pointing. "Come on, I'll show you. My horse is right over there in the shade of that tree."

Freddy was a pretty good horseman, even at his age, Chappie noticed, as they were riding along side by side on the road.

"So, Freddy, how long have you been working with pigs? It's a pretty smelly job, if you ask me."

"This is my first time, and the smell isn't really that bad after you been around them a couple three days. Last year I got a job herding cattle for Mr. Henberry. I don't take much to milking cows, but, my brother is still working there, milking. I guess he doesn't mind it."

"Max seems like a nice, capable feller. You look a lot like him." Changing the subject, Chappie added, "You handle that horse real well. You should go some place where they appreciate good riders. I know a couple of people down in the valley that need a good cowboy. Maybe I could make a recommendation for you, if you're interested."

"Gee, thanks, mister, but my parents say I'm too young yet to take off on my own."

"Well, keep it in mind. I'll be there when, or if, you decide to come down there."

"I want to go back east to school. My parents are from Pennsylvania, and they said there were some good schools back there where a feller could learn how to do things and become successful in life. I'd like to know how they made them train engines and the tracks they run on. I read all about that railroad after they had that ceremony at Promontory Point, and I'd just like to know how the heck they can make something like that. I've just about got enough money saved up to ride that thing."

"It sounds like you've pretty well made up your mind about that, and I'll tell you, them trains are the coming thing. I hear they're laying tracks about everywhere, and pretty soon they'll be going all over the country. Everybody will be able to hop on a train and travel just about anywhere they want faster than they've ever done it before. It's going to put the stagecoaches out of business, mark my words." There was no response from the young lad, so he continued, "I think that's a mighty smart decision on your part, but don't tell your mother I said that."

Freddy grinned at that, and decided he was beginning to like this feller from the valley. He talks my kind of language, he thought.

"You can tie your horse up right there at the hitch rail and just knock on the front door. I'm going to take this one around to the barn," Freddy said, when they reached the house.

Chappie did as told, that is, he was in the act of tying the horse's reins to the rail when the front door opened and Mrs. Proudmire stepped out onto the porch.

"Well, well, Mr. Wesford, to what do we owe this honor? Come in, come in. I was just setting the table for dinner, and you're welcome to join us, if you'd care to."

I passed a pleasant repast with the Proudmires, but didn't learn anything knew or interesting that wasn't already known or surmised.

CHAPTER 8

I headed back to town over the same road I had traveled before, since it was the only wagon road that seemed to take that direction. I could've probably returned over the hills on an animal trail, but I had no good reason to sneak around. It'll be around sunset when I get to town, and that'll be fine.

Cramer was drawing a beer for somebody I didn't know as I entered the saloon after putting my horse in Cranky's small stable. His buggy was gone.

"There you go, Henry, enjoy," Cranky said, setting the glass on the bar in front of the customer. "Hey, Chappie, that Milt's been looking for you. He seemed awful upset again, too. Don't know why. This gentleman is Henry Dugan. Henry shake hands with Chappie Wesford from down in the valley."

The two men shook hands and exchanged howdys, as Cramer continued prattling, "Henry owns some cattle and runs a ranch over to the west a few miles. Ain't that right, Henry? You drinking anything, Chappie?"

"Nah, but if you had some kind of cooking facility here, I'd buy myself something to eat. I'm getting hungry."

"People come in here to drink, not eat, and who would do the cooking? I don't have no time for it. Have to go to a lot of expense to do that, and might sell one or two meals a month, and the Indians would be in here begging for food every night. Don't need that kind of aggravation. Bad enough cleaning up after you and Milt," he said with a chuckle.

"What do you think, Henry?" asked Wesford. "Would you spend any money on food, if Cranky had something to eat now and then?"

"Maybe, but I doubt it. It's hard enough to have a little beer money, let alone waste it on food that I can get at home. I don't come in here that often anyway."

"See, see! That's the attitude of the local people," said Cramer in an irritated tone. "Never have any money for anything, but they all got the latest gadget at home. You can bet on that!"

"Now, Cranky, don't go getting all upset about it. You know how farming and ranching is, never getting ahead and hard to keep up," Henry explained. "Besides, ain't no place for a good church man to be....in here. You know if it wasn't for us thirsty ones, you wouldn't have no business, anyway."

"Don't go getting me started on religion," Cranky said, "'cause it ain't settled nothing since its creation. Why, you know its...it's...always, oh, the hell with it! Chappie, watch the bar a minute, will you?" And Cranky disappeared into the back room.

"I think he's mellowing a bit, since the last time I was in town," said Henry, taking a long, slow sip of beer, like he wanted it to last awhile, smacking his lips and savoring the taste. "Ah-ah-um," he sighed.

Chappie didn't say anything for two or three minutes, and Henry sat on the bar stool staring at his beer, like it was going to reveal some great secret or get up and run away. Henry hoisted the nearly empty glass to his lips again, and finished it in the same fashion as before, smacking his lips together, letting out a long groan of satisfaction, "Ah-aah-um," and sat the glass back on the bar.

"Well, my wife ought to be about done at the store. He might already be closed and she'll be sitting in the wagon, waiting for me to show up to cuss me out about drinking and spending hard-earned money on the devil's work. She had to come to town and get some baking soda to make biscuits with. Couldn't wait 'til Saturday. Just had to do it. That ever happen to you?"

"All the time, but you got to keep them happy, if you're ever to have any peace at home," Chappie answered, although he wasn't married.

Cranky returned to the bar area with a plate of food, setting it down in front of Chappie saying, "Here's a bite for you, since you're so awful hungry, bread and bacon."

"By golly, Cranky! You didn't have to do that. I could've eat some beef jerky, but this looks better. Thanks!"

"You owe me a dollar for it, the stable, and a place to sleep!"

"Whoa, now! Hold on there! I didn't ask for none of it, so how come I owe you a dollar?"

"'Cause I said so, that's why! And that's it, no dollar - no food and bunk!"

"You sure drive a hard bargain, don't he, Henry? In the first place, I ain't sure I got a dollar. If I don't, can I owe it to you? That bacon looks real good with that bread."

There was the sound of horses pounding to a stop outside amid yelling and laughing, and in came the three Henberry brothers, Jim, Oakley, and Milt, and the two milkers, Mike and Wonder.

"I'll see you, Cranky, I think I hear the wife calling!" Henry said, and left in a hurry.

"Set them up there, Cranky! We're all drinking whiskey tonight!" yelled Milt. "No! By golly, we'll set at that table at the open end of the bar so you don't have to walk so far. Just bring us a bottle of any kind whiskey!" he yelled.

"I think you owe me something from the last time, Milt. Your Pa only paid me a few dollars for all that damage you did, and I haven't been able to get it all repaired. Five dollars ought to do it, and three dollars for the whiskey."

Milt stared at Cranky like he didn't understand what he had said. "Pa said he settled up with you, fair and square, for everything. Come on, now, give us that whiskey!"

"Maybe one of your brothers will pay something toward it. How about it Jim, Oakley?"

"Tell you what, Cranky," Chappie broke in. "I feel partly responsible for the damages, even though I wasn't here 'til later, so I'll chip in two dollars for that and a dollar for some rotgut, if they'll make up the difference."

The newcomers huddled around the table, whispering, until Jim spoke up, "We'd like to know what brings him to think that he has to buy a drink for the Henberrys?"

It got so quiet you could hear the horses snuffling outside, but no one made any hasty movements.

Cranky said, "Chappie, I didn't think you had any money, the way you were talking before."

"I don't know what's so difficult about paying for something that I may have been partly the cause of, and in the interest of trying to settle up or heal something that might have been misunderstood, I just want to do my part. If you and they don't want to accept my offer, so be it."

"Stranger, I don't know what your business is here," put in Mike, the milker, "but I'm ready to accept your offer, and I'll throw in a dollar for whiskey, too. I'm beginning not to hate this feller too much."

"I was wondering if I could put in a quarter, too," chimed in Wonder.

Jim looked at Chappie then Oakley and Milt, and added, "I think we're going to drink that whiskey and forget the past, right Milt? And here is two dollars, that's enough for the whiskey. Set it up, Cranky!"

"I still want to know what he's snooping around here for, asking all those questions about everybody. I don't trust him at all," said Milt, with a sneer.

"Gentlemen, gentlemen, if you can just put aside your feelings and anger 'til after the big celebration day after tomorrow, we don't want to ruin anybody's Fourth of July now, do we?" Chappie said. "Right now, let's all have a drink of that sagebrush juice to celebrate!"

Cranky poured some whiskey into a small glass for Chappie at the bar and then put the bottle on the table for the others. Nobody asked Chappie to join them at the table, as they began whispering, everybody at once, then Wonder said, "I wonder what's up his sleeve," and they all broke into loud laughter.

Chappie ignored them and ate his bacon and bread finally, and chased it with a glass of beer. He was watching Cramer wipe down the bar, wash a couple of glasses, and walk from one end of the bar to the other then back again. Cranky finally turned around and arranged some bottles on the shelf behind, then went and struck a match to the three kerosene lamps, one hanging by the front door and one at each end of the bar.

The door opened, and in walked Bishop Thorneycraft and Counselor Carlson. The men at the table stopped whispering. Chappie turned around as Cranky with a surprised look stared at the new customers all dressed up in suits and ties.

"By golly!" Cranky exclaimed. "If it ain't the Bishop and Mr. Carlson. Howdy-do, gentlemen. What'll it be, sarsaparilla? And what brings you gents in tonight?"

Thorneycraft looked at his assistant, then surveyed the group of men at the table, looked at Cramer, finally rested his eyes on Chappie.

"Evening, gentlemen. Counselor and I saw all the horses out front as we left my house, so we came by to see what the occasion was, in addition to doing our duties for the town. We're glad you're all here so we can ask you to spread our message this evening, which is, as most of you may already know, ahem....is our annual Fourth of July Celebration. We're hoping that everyone around comes into town to enjoy themselves and take part in the church picnic in the field behind the church building under the trees. We announced it in church last Sunday, but we didn't say anything about a special guest coming to town to help us celebrate. So we ask that you all take this message home and tell everyone you meet."

Turning his attention to the barkeep, he continued, "And, Mr. Cramer, we've come to present a petition to you on behalf of everyone who signed it to please stop selling hard liquors and beer to our citizens. The wives have been complaining that their husbands spend too much time and money on your evil, spirituous libations and come home drunk too many times. And you will see as you read it, that not only wives have signed it, but husbands, too,....ahem....in some cases, and even a couple of Utes have put there marks. And, I'd like to add on behalf of all the righteous citizens of this town, that the church must protest the continued practice of serving hard liquors and may be looking to force the shut-down of your establishment if such practice continues. And, with that, we'll take a non-alcoholic drink of some kind. Thank you!"

Chappie stood up and applauded, and everyone joined in, even Cranky.

"Mighty fine speech, Bishop!" said Chappie. "Any idea who this special guest is going to be?"

"I don't rightly know, Chappie, but there's a rumor flying around that started with the feller that drives the mail wagon, Angus MacDougald. He said he heard something about a big uppity-up coming to Utah Territory for something or other. Didn't rightly know who or what or when. Said he could be coming any day, though. That's all I know."

Jim Henberry spoke up, "Pa was talking about some darn politician coming to Utah that he read in the papers he gets, but said the feller's name sure wasn't familiar to him. Didn't say a thing about coming here, though."

"Why would one of them people want to be coming to Altveel for? I'll bet you it's something to do with the Ute tribe. That's what it always is!" Oakley said.

This set all the men to talking among themselves, and Chappie found it hard to get a word in edgewise, but he didn't have anything to add, anyway. He watched as Cramer set an old bottle labeled Sarsaparilla Made From the Finest Old Recipe Available" on the bar for Thorney and Carlson with two glasses. He thought it looked suspiciously like good malt and barley whiskey, but he knew that they wouldn't drink any hard liquor, not even after dark.

He glanced at the one front window and caught little Charlie's eye before the boy ducked out of sight. About five minutes later, Esther Bigknife came in the front door. Conversation stopped, as she looked around the room glancing from one hat to another, finally resting her pretty, dark eyes on Cranky. She said, "Thanks for the use of your buggy, Cranky. I put it back in the stable." Then turning her attention to Milt after a quick glance at Chappie said, "Milt, I've got some fresh-made oyster stew waiting, if you'd care to help Charlie and me eat it. Sorry, gents, I only got enough for us three."

"Now, Esther, you know I'm drinking with the boys, and...," Milt began, but Jim interrupted, saying, "Widow Bigknife, if you're trying to keep Milt from causing a ruckus tonight, you don't have to worry about that, does she Milt? We're heading out as soon as we finish our drinks, ain't that right, boys?"

Oakley and Wonder shook their heads up and down in the affirmative, Milt and Mike just sat there watching Esther.

The Bishop thought he had better say something, so he spoke up, "Mrs. Bigknife, you can see we're just having a friendly drink to celebrate our upcoming holiday and the fact that there'll be a special visitor coming to town to help with it. Why don't you have a sarsaparilla with us? Cranky, put a glass up here for Mrs. Bigknife."

"If she's going to give that stew to that feller later," pointing at Chappie, "I'm going to go eat it," said Milt, rising up from the table.

"Why would she do that?" asked Chappie. "I just ate some bacon and bread and I'm full, and just finishing my drink before I help the Bishop and the Counselor deliver the news."

"I don't believe that feller for a minute," Milt said. "Where's he staying, anyway?"

Chappie was growing a little tired of Milt's attitude. He stood up, looked directly at Milt, and said, "I don't believe it's any concern of yours where I pitch my tent, Mr. Henberry. If you're having a little trouble accepting my presence in town, maybe you ought to try running me out!"

This put a burr under Milt's saddle and he came at Chappie in a rush, but Esther stepped in between them before he had gotten very far.

"Milt! Stop! Chappie, quit egging him on! Don't you men have any sense at all?" she yelled.

"Get out of my way, Esther!" Milt ordered. "I'm going to teach him a lesson he'll never forget! He'll never want to come back here!"

"No, I ain't going to move! Say something, Chappie, to make him sit down!" she pleaded.

The Bishop spoke instead, "Gentlemen! Gentlemen! You've tore up Cranky's place too many times now. Why don't you take it outside before he gets his shotgun? And you, Milt, did your Pa put you up to this again? You been chasing all the newcomers away for quite awhile, and I think it's because your Pa don't want anybody to move in on him! Ain't that right?"

Milt, Jim, and Oakley stared at the Bishop like he had committed a grievous sin.

"Them outsiders come into town and start snooping around, asking a lot of questions, and first thing you know they have the whole town spreading gossip and talking, and Pa don't like that," Milt said. "And he don't want no outsider trying to take over his land, neither, making trouble for the family."

"I'll admit some of the farmers and their wives, mostly the womenfolk, talk about you," the Bishop said, "but it ain't like they thought this stuff up themselves, with all the drinking and carousing and fighting you boys do around town, but the outsiders don't cause all that."

Oakley put his two cents in, "We don't like outsiders, so let Milt finish his business with this one! Take him outside Milt and let him know what a Henberry is made of!"

"There ain't no need for that, is there Milt?" Chappie said. "With the big celebration coming up, I challenge you to a match in front of the church on the Fourth of July. No holds barred. And we'll see just who is the better man! There ain't nobody going to chase me out of town."

"That's it, Milt!" said Jim. "You can beat him at wrestling or a fighting match. That's a good idea to my way of thinking."

And Oakley, Wonder and Mike agreed, chiming in, "Yahoo! That's a good idea! We ain't never had a match like that around here!"

"Well, well," said the Bishop. "What's it to be Milt? Although the church is not the proper place for such an event, we can overlook it one time, can't we Counselor?" thinking this would be a feather in his cap for winning the job as Mayor again when the time for elections rolled around.

Milt relaxed, looked at Esther, and went back to the men gathered around the table at the end of the bar, where they huddled in a conference talking in low tones.

Esther gazed at Chappie, then Cranky, then the Bishop and his Councilor, and then at Milt, who had his back toward her. She didn't say anything, but she thought, "I don't want either one to get hurt. I'm beginning to like Chappie almost too much. Every time I see him, I get that fluttering in my chest and it's hard to breathe until it wears off. I haven't had those feelings in a long time. And poor dear Milt, I don't want to see him hurt either."

It was quiet in the tavern except for the buzzing of the Henberry cowboys, and there was electricity in the air as the bystanders waited for the big decision, not saying a word or even taking a drink, except Chappie. He stared into the eyes of Esther until she turned away, then he sat down on his stool and lifted his glass and drained the last sip of whiskey, licking his lips and not paying attention, or so it seemed, to the men at the end of the bar. He relaxed and smiled at Esther as she turned her gaze back to him.

She wondered what was going through his mind, as her thoughts raced around in her head, worried about Milt. Then she worried about the man from the valley. Again, she hoped nothing bad happened to him, either. She had begun to like the way he looked at her, and she knew his concern for Charlie was genuine. If she had been a "nice lady," she felt she might have a chance with him, but not now.

The buzz from the table grew louder, and then stopped all together, as Milt turned around and announced his decision.

"Bishop Thorneycraft," he began and looked at Esther, then Chappie, "you can tell that stranger from the valley, that I choose hands, fists, and muscles for the match on the Fourth, and we'll settle this once and for all," and a broad grin appeared on his dark face, and his companions let out a big roar of approval.

"'At a boy, Milt!" said Jim. "You can take him for sure."

"Okay, men, okay," Thorneycraft said. "What does the valley man have to say to this?"

They all settled down as Wesford got up from his stool. He looked at Esther, who seemed to be holding her breath, then the church men and Cranky, then the Henberry group and finally at Milt, and a wide grin exposing his even white teeth crossed his face as he said, "Thorney, tell the Henberry gentleman and his brothers and friends that it will be my pleasure to make him cry uncle on the Fourth of July, and a hip-hip-hooray for the Territory, hooray for the Nation, and a special hooray for Mrs. Bigknife, Charlie, and the small town of Altaveel! Hip-hip-hooray?" he yelled.

This was met with stunned silence as his cheers sank in, then loud hoo-rays could be heard as far away as the Fedderson house a half-mile down the road.

Cal Fedderson turned to his wife and said, "Did you hear that, Barb, they must've started celebrating the Fourth early this year down at the saloon."

CHAPTER 9

The news traveled fast and wide in the small town, everybody was talking about the big match coming up, and some bets were being placed among friends and even enemies. There hadn't been an event like this that anyone had ever heard of before, and it was sure to be a grand celebration. There was even talk that the Bishop had a hand in it, and had offered the church property for the match.

Preparations had been underway for the regular celebration, but now it was going to be an even bigger affair, especially for the male gender of the community. The females were not too thrilled about two men knocking their heads together just to see who was the toughest, but there were some who were getting a tingle of excitement about the upcoming spectacle, hoping that someone would finally tame Milt Henberry and with it the entire Henberry clan. Esther was caught between a rock and a hard place over it, because her two favorite men were going to test their strength and fighting skills against each other. Oh, worry, worry.

Adding to the widespread, and for the most part, happy hullabaloo was the news about the special guest coming to town. Everyone had their own idea who it was going to be, and kept a sharp eye on the road into town from the valley to be the first to get a glimpse of the illustrious personage, whoever it may be.

The local grade school musicians, eight in number, had been practicing in the afternoons for the past few weeks, even though school was closed, a rendition of a popular marching song, and hoped to have it mastered on time. Mrs. Nelson, the music teacher, was to the point of pulling out her gray hair until the uncoordinated noise suddenly began sounding more like music, and she decided to push a little harder.

Chappie, though, had other things to attend to, including a lot of traveling around in the short time remaining. He parleyed with the elder Jim Henberry for most of the following morning, and even a short bit with Milt, and then he had to go back to town and talk with Mrs. Bigknife, then Cal Fedderson, again, and Proudmire, who was in town with the family shopping for the big celebration. He stopped at the general store to pick up some shaving soap and heard some more rumors and innuendo about "poor little Charlie and that Widow Bigknife" from the some of the town's citizens. He had a private conference with Bishop Thorneycraft at the church, the last thing before he returned to his camp in the hills. It was already dark.

Daylight was just beginning to make the cedar trees visible when there were two booms heard over the entire hilly area. Cal jumped out of bed saying to his wife, "Good grief, honey, they're celebrating already! I hope they didn't blow up the church. I'm going to take a look out the window."

Widow Bigknife was shocked out of her sleep, too, and Charlie came running in to her room yelling, "Ma! Ma! What they doing? I think they broke our windows!"

"It's just the older boys setting off dynamite, Charlie, to start the Fourth of July celebration. Let's get dressed and see what's going on."

And it was like that all over town, causing lamps to be lighted and fires in stoves to be rekindled, and farmers, wives, and their kids to crawl out of bed and get ready for the day. By the time the sun had barely climbed above the eastern peaks, kids were playing ante-aye-over and chasing each other around the church, and the older ones were lighting firecrackers and making all the noise they could muster. Someone had scattered colored paper and streamers all over the store, the hitch rails, and the fences along the road. There were already two wagons tied up to the fence near the saloon and more plodding into town. At the other end, where the road turns north by the church, more wagons and buggies were looking for a place to tie up. There was a big fire going in the vacant lot in front of the church with some people standing around it taking off the chill, and kids asking their mothers between runs around the fire when they were going to eat breakfast.

A group of farmers stood back a few feet behind the women, talking about the upcoming match and placing even more wagers on the man they had picked to win. "I heard that man from the valley was a heavyweight champion boxer," one said. "Heck no! Who told you that? That Milt Henberry can lick any man standing, he can. He's one tough son-of-a-gun!" "I got three dollars he ain't no match for that valley man!" And back and forth it went, until some broke away from the group and started small fires on which they planned to cook their meat and eggs. Their wives followed and brought the utensils and broke some eggs into the frying pan and cooked their bacon and biscuits, yelling at their towheads to get a plate from the wagon and come get your food.

At the lone camp out of town behind the hills, Chappie had heard the two blasts, but they weren't quite loud enough to wake him. He didn't need them to arouse him, as he was just lying there going over in his head the speech he was going to attempt later in the day. He never gave his upcoming fight a thought; he was more worried, no that wasn't the word, entangled is better, entangled in the wording of his speechifying. Once he got it going, he knew he would be just fine, because it was always the first part that ruined many a speech, at least in his mind.

He sat up and clasped his arms around his knees, tightening and loosening the hard muscles of his arms and legs, then stretching his legs out on the ground and spreading them as far as he could. He stood up and threw his arms to the right, then the left, and bent down and touched his toes, straightened back up and commenced gathering his outfit together. Chappie walked over to his horse, reached down and picked up a handful of oats from the feedbag on the ground and fed it to him.

Returning to the campfire, now out, he quickly had it going and a small pot of water heating. When he thought it was hot enough, he removed it from the fire, set it on the ground, and hunkered down by it. Taking a mirror out of his bag, he adjusted it on a rock so he could see his reflection, sharpened his razor, and lathered his face with a brush and the newly bought small bar of shaving soap, then commenced shaving the whiskers that had grown since he had shaved last, which were almost long enough to cut with the scissors.

After he was finished shaving, he packed everything up and tied it on to his horse, even the bag which held his clothes. He put out the fire and scattered the ashes around in the dirt to make sure they wouldn't catch fire again. Surveying the site where his camp had been, he was satisfied that he had returned it to its natural state, as if no one had been there. He climbed atop Spottie, making sure his bag, bedroll and saddlebags were evenly distributed and secure, and said, "Giddy-up, Spottie, let's get it over with."

As he went up the road toward the town, he could hear firecrackers and a lot of yelling and loud laughing. Chappie turned onto the road through town, passing the Bishop's store, which was doing a good business with three or four wagons in front, and people going in and coming out. He thought, "Thorney must have hired some help to keep the store open today, because the Bishop had to be at the church and ceremonies all day, probably." He stopped his horse, got off, and walked up near the front window so he could see his reflection. It was a little distorted, and he couldn't get a very good look, but he thought he appeared quite handsome and satisfied for the time being. Ah, vanity!

Climbing back on Spottie, he urged the horse to a slow trot, and kept it up until he reached the saloon, where he put Spottie in the stable by Cranky's buggy and horses. He untied the bag with his clothes and carried it with him. The back door to the tavern was open, so he went in quietly as possible. There were noises from the bar area of the cowboys and farmers talking and laughing and making bets. They'll be in fine fettle by the time the ceremonies begin, thought Chappie. Putting his bag on Cranky's bunk, he quickly removed his boots, pants and shirt and donned his old Union Army uniform with the Colonel insignia on the shoulders, the rank to which he had been promoted at the end of the war. Too bad he didn't have a mirror big enough in which he could take another look at himself, to see how everything fit. He would've liked to have been able to make sure that everything was in order. He was surprised that he could still button the pants, and the jacket still fit good, although snug.

Not making any more noise than he had to, he put some water in the coffee pot, and found the coffee grounds and poured enough in for some good strong coffee, and rekindled the fire in the small stove. He sat down at the table and made himself comfortable as possible, put on his Army hat, pulling it down over his forehead, waiting for the coffee to boil.

Cranky came through the door to the bar and stopped when he saw the soldier sitting at the table. "What the... who the...what the...devil you doing in here?"

Chappie raised his head, "It's just me, Cranky! I needed a place to change my clothes. Don't say anything to those farmers out there. I'm enjoying a few minutes of peace and quiet before I go to the ceremonies, and having a sip of coffee. Hope you don't mind."

"So you're the special guest, huh? All dressed up in uniform! Why didn't you say something? By golly,

Chappie, if I'd known that, I would've given you better accommodations, you could've had my bunk!"

"You did fine, Cranky, and I appreciate it, and will reimburse you for the food and stuff. What are you looking for?"

"I just came in to make myself some coffee. I got to have something to put up with all the people today. Thanks for making it."

"Well, I'm supposed to show up around ten or eleven to make my speech. So, I'll just sit here for awhile, and don't tell anybody for Pete's sake! I'll be bothered enough without starting with it here. I'm going to leave my stuff here until afterwards."

"Don't you worry, Chappie, your secret is good as gold with me. Let me grab a cup of that stuff and I'll leave you alone. Good luck, today! My money is on you to cut Milt down to size."

Chappie enjoyed his time alone, and after saying a short prayer, he went out and climbed on Spottie for the short ride to the festivities. A wagon full of children all decorated with flags of one kind or another and paper ribbons flowing from the horses' backs was coming from the church. He stopped to watch it, and the kids saw him and started cheering. He could see little Charlie among them waving his arms and yelling with the others. The driver was old Proudmire, with a big grin on his face. Chappie raised his right arm and saluted, and waited for the wagon to pass, and the boys and girls to see something else to cheer about.

He urged Spottie to a slow trot and kept it up until he reached the picnic grounds, where he tied up to the top rail of the old fence near the gate, squeezing in between wagons. "That one is the one we pulled out of the creek," he murmured. He started walking to the nearest table, but didn't get far. Ole Thorneycraft had spied him tying up, and came walking toward him, and some more kids had also seen him and came running to see the man in uniform, running around and yelling silly questions.

"Leave the man alone, Bobby and Billy!" the Bishop yelled. "You kids go on and play out in the field." Looking at Chappie, he said, "By jiggers, General Wesford, you're sure making an impression in that uniform. Folks around here ain't seen too many soldiers all dressed up."

More people started gathering around, including the Feddersons and the Proudmire wife, and others he didn't know yet. They were all talking about the feller in the uniform, who is he? Is he that dignitary from Washington everybody was talking about, the big politician? Is he the special guest we heard about?

"Just a Colonel, Bishop, at your service," said Chappie.

"Why, it's Mr. Wesford from the valley, Calvin," said Barbara Fedderson. "What's he doing all dressed up? Is he going to make a speech?"

"I don't know, Barb. He's just talking with Bishop Thorneycraft right now. That uniform sure brings back memories. He's a full Colonel! I'll be darned!"

"Gentlemen, gentlemen!" shouted the Bishop, "and ladies, too! Give us room! Make way for the Gen-rul! Make way for the Gen-rul! Quiet, everybody! Quiet, please! I think he wants to say something! Quiet!"

Chappie looked at the crowd and then Thorneycraft, and said, "I would like some breakfast, Thorney, if anyone has some food. I'm starved right now."

About everyone spoke up, "Come with us! Come to our table, we'll feed you good!"

Chappie surveyed the crowd and settled his gaze on the Feddersons and said, "Thanks everybody, thanks! But Mrs. Fedderson says she has breakfast about ready? Ain't that right Cal?"

"You bet it is! Right over here, Colonel!"

Hilaine grabbed his arm on one side and Barbara on the other and led him to their setup under a tree with a crowd following along behind.

"Just grab a plate and we'll load it up for you!" said Hilaine.

"By golly, this is an honor, a real honor to have a full Colonel eat a bite with us, huh, Barbara? I had no idea that you're in the Army, Chappie," said Cal.

"I was recalled to active duty for a while and given the temporary rank of Colonel, having been recommended by some high church authorities and selected by the new General in charge of the Army here in Utah, for the purpose of providing some patriotic formalities to some of the Fourth of July celebrations. And that's the long explanation for my appearance in uniform."

"You certainly look impressive, Mr. Wesford, doesn't he Darlena?" said Hilaine. "How many eggs do you want?"

"Well, your just showing up here and asking a lot of questions has caused some people to wonder what the heck's it all about?" said Cal. "And rumor has it that somebody took a shot at you to keep you from finding out too much. Do you know who it was, Chappie?"

"I have a pretty good idea, but I'm not ready to disclose it."

"How do you like those fried taters? It's my secret seasoning that makes them taste that way," said Darlena, who had been doing the breakfast cooking. "Come on, Freddy, you better eat some, and Josh, quit playing around," she yelled at her young cousin.

"Here comes Aunt Bessie!" said Freddy, and he left to talk to Brigham Proudmire.

"We had to get a close look at the man in uniform, Barb!" Bessie greeted them. "I knew it was Mr. Wesford! I even told Roger it was, but he didn't believe it. My! My! Isn't he handsome?"

And the morning went passing by.

Bishop Thorneycraft (or Mayor Thorneycraft, whichever hat he was wearing today) pulled his watch out of the vest pocket in which it had been resting, studied the numbers for at least 15 or 20 seconds, then raised his right hand to the sky, yelling "Ladies and gentlemen! It's time for the ceremonies to begin!" and lowered the arm to point at the little band which had assembled quickly on the church steps.

Mrs. Nelson raised her arms and said "All right, children," and lowered them to start the music, which was immediately blasted out all out of tune. And then, an amazing thing happened. It all came together and sounded almost perfect to her ears, as she motioned with her arms and shook her head up and down, "That's it! That's it, children! Good! Good!"

And the music blasted out over the crowd, and everybody started singing along, except the teen-aged boys, who were setting off firecrackers and running around, shouting and clapping their hands. The ceremony was off to a slam-bang start.

The Henberry brothers had heard about the man in uniform, and tried to edge in and get a closer look to make sure it was who everybody said it was. Wesford was standing next to the Bishop/Mayor on the lower step below the band, so they couldn't get too close, but Oakley told his brothers, "It was that Wesford feller all right. I saw him earlier with the Feddersons."

The church janitor had removed the chairs from the church, and set them up in rows. There were only enough for 35 or 40 people, and the elder Mr. Henberry and his wife were sitting in the front row. They got a clear view of the proceedings taking place and the school kids playing the music.

Little Charlie was peeking out between two women standing adjacent to the chairs, and his mother was barely visible in the back fringes standing by herself. Roger Proudmire was a few feet from her standing on a table to see over the crowd. There were more farmers, wives, and ranch hands standing around the fringes, some of the young men on tops of the tables, more folks than there were sitting on the chairs. There were some Ute Indians in a group watching the "crazy" white people's pow-wow from a short distance away among the trees, including Long Paul and Flat Paul.

Milt Henberry was not too far from Esther, either, but his mind was on other things. Seeing Wesford show up in uniform and knowing now that he was the high-faluting dignitary for today's celebration, had given him cause to think about who it was he was actually going to beat up later. Maybe he had been a bit hasty in accepting the challenge. If the high church authorities and the newspapers ever got wind of this, he'd be in big trouble, especially with his Pa. His Pa wouldn't want him to be ruining any business proposition that may come along later. "Darn! What am I going to do?" he worried.

Young Jim and Oakley Henberry were now at the front, way to the side of the crowd, watching the band playing through the notes. Oakley had a worried look, thinking he had almost shot the bigwig, and he and Milt had gone after him, too. There would be hell to pay and a lot of explaining if they had succeeded. He wondered what was going to be the outcome of it. Would they be arrested and thrown in jail, or what? It was going to ruin my plans for marrying Hilaine Fedderson, he thought. Darn it! Why didn't I just hold off until I knew what was going on?

Young Jim was thinking that he knew "that feller" was somebody important, but he went along with his brothers anyway. He thought, "I should have stopped them, but I didn't."

And others in the crowd had their own ideas about the man in uniform, including Esther Bigknife, little Charlie, the Fedderson sisters and husbands, Big Mike, Wonder, and even that Mr. Lupadakis, whose wagon he helped dislodge from the creek. And then there was Cranky Cramer, who had closed his saloon so he could come and see what his old acquaintance had to say. He had sure changed since Cramer knew him as a young man down in the valley. And Roger Proudmire, standing on a table trying to spot Barbara Fedderson in the crowd with his wife, hoping he could see her alone for awhile.

There was a noisy hooray from the crowd and a lot of applause as the band hit the final note of the piece and

Mrs. Nelson dropped her arms and let out a big sigh of happy relief, amazed that the kids had played so well.

The Bishop shouted, "Fine work! Fine work, kids! Beautiful! We'll do it again in a few minutes! Thank you, thank you! Thank you, Mrs. Nelson?" The crowd became quiet except for a firecracker or two going off, and the Bishop started again, "Now, ladies and gentlemen! I would like to say a few words on the meaning of this celebration and this great country's rise to glory, and.... etc.....etc......" and on and on he went making another speech to get himself re-elected, until he came to the part that went "and now, ladies and gentlemen, and Mrs. Nelson and the band, can we have a little musical introduction to honor our special guest?" There was applause and shouting, and laughter from the crowd as a cowboy yelled, "Get on with it, Bishop, it'll be dark in a few hours, ha-ha-ha!"

The band began playing the same song again, out of tune of course, until they had played a few bars, then picked up correctly just in time to be stopped.

"That'll do! That'll do, Mrs. Nelson! Thank you, thank you!" the Bishop said. "And now, friends and neighbors, ladies and gentlemen, and everybody else, ahem, as Mayor of this town it is my great and distinct pleasure to introduce the special guest of the day....in a moment or two. But first, I would like to say that it has been extremely difficult keeping it secret. I was told that a very important official would be in town for the Fourth, but I didn't know his name, and when he showed up, I still wasn't sure that he was the fellow. However, he made it clear to me two or three days ago that he was, indeed, that gentleman. Let me tell you a little about him, if I may. He's a veteran of the Union Army, now the United States Army, and participated in several engagements with the Indians and in the Civil War, and he is now a United States Marshal for Utah Territory in addition to being a General ...woops, I've just been corrected. He says he is a Colonel, not a General, but I hope he don't mind if I continue calling him General. And so, it is my great honor, to introduce to those who haven't already made his acquaintance, General Chappie Wesford! Let's give him a warm Altveel welcome!"

And the band started up again amid all the shouting and blasting firecrackers, and the surprise and consternation of the Henberry brothers, who became nervous and fidgety and broke out in sweat upon hearing that this "feller" was a U.S. Marshal. The man in the Union Army uniform stepped up a couple of steps on the front porch, where he could see over the applauding crowd.

"Ladies and gentlemen! Ladies and gentlemen!" he began as the folks slowly stopped clapping. "It has been my pleasure to spend the last few days in your town meeting some of the residents. I was recalled to Army service for a few days and had to relinquish my duties as a Marshal for a brief period, having been commissioned as a Colonel, to come to Altaveel, or as you say, Altveel, to conduct a brief ceremony, which I will get to pronto.

"But, first I would like to say a little bit about some of the local citizens I have had the pleasure to meet since my surreptitious arrival. I took a tour of the biggest dairy farm, that of the elder James Henberry, and visited his grist mill, the cheese factory, a pig farm of Mr. Proudmire, and yes, I've even broken one of the restrictions of our religion by visiting the local tavern and having a beer with Mr. Cramer, for which I hope I will be forgiven. Cranky and I go back a long ways, having met quite a few years ago when I was merely a young lad and the valley had just been opened for settlement. I enjoyed rehashing old times, even though I've had to take matters into my own hands on a couple of occasions at the bar, one of which has led to a prospective fighting match with one of the Henberry sons and myself. I saw the small dam in Little Mouth Canyon on the creek that runs through town, ate some fresh blackberries right off the vine, and assisted in the removal of a wagon from the creek with Mr. Proudmire. I've had a couple of meetings with Bishop Thorneycraft, the Mayor, and took a look in his store. And it's all been a pleasure, indeed, this break from hunting down some of the worst elements of society and putting them behind bars.

"And before we get on with the ceremony, I would like to add a note on the personal stories of a couple of your residents. I've spent some time with a lady of the town who is not very well looked on by the more religious and virtuous of the citizens here, although I am at a loss to understand their feelings. Esther Bigknife and her son Charlie have faced some hard times in their lives and this town, and I hope what I'm about to say will make their lives a little easier than it has been."

There was a general murmuring that ran through the crowd from all the whispering and a comment or two that could be heard. "What business is it of his?" "Who's he talking about, what religious people?" "Does he think I'm one of those?" "He didn't come here to lecture us on morals, did he?" Etc. Etc.

Chappie waited until the noise died, then continued, as if he hadn't been interrupted, "This lady and her first husband relocated to this beautiful spot in the hills from Kansas City when this area was just being settled, and as the result of hard luck on his part and not really knowing enough of the cattle business, they went bust. The loss was too much to bear for the husband who saw fit to kill himself up in Skunk Pass, and this young woman was left to struggle on her own. What I'm about to tell you is something that has been kept under the rug all these years, and in and of itself is something that people may not look on too highly, but I don't think it should be frowned on in this day and age. The lady later got remarried, this time to a Ute Indian named Charlie Bigknife who also came to a tragic end, and here she was again struggling along trying to make a living for herself and the child soon to be born.

"But there is a hero and a villain in this story as it unfolds. Widow Bigknife soon became the talk of the town among the young cowboys, and her oyster stew became quite famous among them. But, we must return to an earlier time after the death of her Kansas husband. There was another person, a benefactor, in her life, the part hero and part villain, who helped her get through this agonizing stage of her life. Some of you may remember that she took a trip back east, supposedly, to visit her family and friends in Kansas. But, friends, she didn't go to Kansas at all, at all. She spent that time in the Great Salt Lake Valley, waiting for the birth of her first child."

Another murmur and rustling went through the crowd, grew louder, then all became quiet again, so quiet

Chappie could hear a meadow lark singing its song from its perch across the road on a fence rail.

"Yes, ladies and gentlemen, she had a child, but she was urged to give it up, and it was adopted by our hero-villain. You see, this feller was already married, but he found out that his wife couldn't have any children. She was barren, they called it, and he weaseled his way into the life of the widow, unbeknownst to anyone else, and became her great friend, and she became with child.

"It was a clever scheme, but his wife was part of it, and she accompanied Widow Bigknife to Great Salt Lake, and the child became a member of that family, and Esther signed a piece of paper saying that she would never disclose the father, and everyone was happy. They all came back here to Altveel and settled down, and Esther later married Charlie the Ute, and had young Charlie, all the while grooming her reputation as, if you will, the town hussy. And, to this day, she has not told anyone who that father is. But, there is another angle to the story. Our hero-villain's wife somehow overcame her barrenness and had more children, and they never left Altaveel, or Altveel, again."

There was a general buzzing through the crowd, everyone trying to guess who the father was. Could it be Roger Proudmire, who had spent a lot of time with Mrs. Bigknife, or even Mr. Fedderson? Cranky Cramer (no, just couldn't be him), even Lupadakis had been seen on more than one occasion back then at her place. Then there was even Bishop Thorneycraft, but knowing how his wife was, that would let him out. Who could it be? Just who was it?

The buzzing slowly died out, as the Bishop raised his right arm, and yelled, "Quiet, Please! Quiet! Let the Gen-rul continue!"

"Well, ladies and gentlemen, I didn't come here for this, but thinking that it would now be in the best interest of those concerned, the town, and Mrs. Bigknife, that everyone knows what the real story is, all parties agreed that I could, and should, tell this story today on the Fourth of July, the birthday of that child, to help them celebrate their blessings!

"But, before I get to that, ladies and gentlemen, I want to say a word or two about Widow Bigknife. Although she never did a thing to change people's minds about her being a woman of ill virtue, and put up with all the insults over the years, none of the bad things that everyone has heard about, or thinks or imagines, happened. And the cowboys and farmers who have visited her only ate her now famous stew, and helped in spreading the word about her bad habits. It was that old situation where they all thought that somebody else had, if you'll pardon my expression, taken advantage of her, they themselves didn't want the others to think that they hadn't also done it. All to make or keep their reputations as men of the world, and the only ones suffering from it were Esther Bigknife and Charlie. But, I am here to tell you now, ladies and gentlemen, that she was a moral woman, just as moral as all the good church ladies of the town, but she did nothing to allay those rumors, only to protect her child that no one knew about. And I've come to like her very much and recognize that she is a beautiful woman. And, if she is in the audience, I'd like her to come up here with me. I have something that I would like to ask her in front of all the townspeople."

This caused a general commotion and louder buzzing and consternation in the crowd as Esther slowly made her way through to the steps. Chappie took her hand and assisted her up them so she didn't fall.

"Quiet! Quiet! Quiet!" shouted the Bishop.

"Well, well, Esther, before I get to my question, I'd like to know if what I have said is true?"

"Yes, Chappie, it's true! All true! And I'm glad now that everything is out in the open."

"Not quite. Would you mind telling us who the father of that baby is? I'm sure he doesn't mind, and who was that baby?"

"It's......it's......Mr. Henberry. The father is Mr. Henberry."

A general roar echoed from the crowd, and if anybody was down at the other end of town, I'm sure they would've heard it.

"Quiet! Quiet! Ladies and gentlemen! Quiet!" the Bishop yelled. "Come on up here, Jim! Come on up here! You might as well be here, too!"

Everyone was trying to get closer, as Henberry mounted the steps.

"Now, Jim! Now, Jim, tell them who that baby was!" said Chappie.

"The baby, of course, was...er...now is Milt, my son Milt!"

"Milt! Come on up here and meet your real mother!" said Chappie.

And there was an even greater uproar from the crowd, and they began to sing, "Happy birthday to you, happy birthday to you......"

Milt finally reached the steps, but he was a little bewildered by all this until Esther put her arms around him and said, "I've waited a long time to do this!"

But Chappie wasn't quite finished. He held up his arms and finally got the crowd quieted down, before he said, "Esther, Esther, will you marry me? .....Hurry up and say yes!"

But he couldn't hear over the shouting of the crowd, as she said, "Yes, yes, I will!" But he grabbed her and hugged her anyway, kissing her on the mouth.

And the people of Altaveel went wild, shooting off firecrackers and yelling and singing, and general cheering. And the band started playing the only tune they knew again.

The Bishop shouted, "Quiet! Quiet!" again, but the noise continued for awhile until it finally died down enough to continue.

"And now, ladies and gentlemen, the ceremony will continue." Turning to Chappie he said, "Chappie! Uh, Gen'rul! If you would, please!"

"All right, if I may. I would like to ask Calvin Fedderson and Roger Proudmire to come up here for a minute. Cal! Roger! If you would? Charlie would you run and get that small satchel from of my horse, Spottie, over there, please."

Charlie was just barely tall enough to reach the knot, but he had it untied in no time and came running back with it to Wesford by the time the two gentlemen made it to the steps.

Asking the Bishop to hold the bag, Chappie reached in and pulled out an envelope.

"Here's my orders, gentlemen." He looked at Fedderson and Proudmire, and continued, "Will you two gents step up a step above us so the people can get a good look at you? That's it, that's better. Now, gentlemen, I have the distinct honor and pleasure to read a short letter given to me by the Territorial General of the Army. It says, 'From the President of the United States.' A loud cheer went up from the crowd. 'It gives me great pleasure and is indeed an honor to sign these citations and present these awards for the courage and bravery above and beyond the call of duty for Roger Proudmire, Corporal, Union Army, and Calvin Fedderson, Private, Union Army, citations enclosed. Signed, Ulysses S. Grant.'

"I will now read the pertinent part of the citations, which states, 'For your actions on the battlefield at Gettysburg in which your bravery, courage, and actions resulted in the saving of many lives that would have otherwise been lost, you are hereby awarded the Civil War Medal of Honor.'"

More cheering from the people of Altaveel.

"I would like to add on my own behalf, that as a company commander of the 280th Pennsylvania Infantry, I witnessed firsthand the bravery and courage on the battlefield that each of you showed that day, that resulted in our being able to retake our positions on the hill and hold them against overwhelming odds. Even though I never met you at Gettysburg, your actions were highly commendable, and it is my great pleasure and duty to give to each of you these awards. Thank you for your bravery and courage."

After draping the medals over their heads, he saluted them, but it took awhile for it to be returned, as both men were astounded by this, and neither one knew that the other had been at Gettysburg. But the crowd was cheering and hurrahing, and the band started up again, and the ceremony was over.

Needless to say, there would be no match that day. Milt didn't feel it would be right to have to beat up his prospective stepfather, whom he had begun to like. And the feud between Proudmire and that dirty ole rascal, Fedderson, was never brought up again, as the two men began talking about Gettysburg and their experiences there and after, and shook hands.

And there was a big crowd of the ladies of the church gathered around the Widow Bigknife to apologize and say how sorry they were for thinking of her that way and welcome her back into the fold.

And Chappie and Esther were married by Mayor, or, Bishop, Thorneycraft, and moved to the valley with Charlie, and were happy. Milt came with them. Oh, yes, they took the painting of Esther and Eddie Jensen along, too.

CHAPTER 10

After all the hub-bub and excitement died down, life returned to some semblance of normality in Altaveel. Cranky's tavern was still open even though he wasn't making as much money as before. The Bishop's store continued serving its customers, and the Bishop was returned to another term as Mayor in the fall by barely defeating Mr. Proudmire and young Oakley Henberry.

Soon after the departure of the newlyweds and Milt, the elder James Henberry called a family meeting after supper one evening, by saying, "Jim, Oakley, and Ma there's something I want to talk to you about."

He glanced around the table to see if he had everyone's attention, and satisfied that he had, he continued, "Oakley, I want you to put your name in the hat for the next election for Mayor."

Everybody spoke at once, "What do you mean, Pa?" said Oakley.

"Mayor! You got to be out of your mind, Pa! Oakley ain't old enough to be a Mayor!" said Jim. "Why not me?"

"Now, Jim......," began Mrs. Henberry.

"Be quiet just a minute, will you, and I'll explain," the elder Henberry began again. "I figure if Oakley can be elected Mayor, we can pretty much run things the way we want around here as far as businesses and controlling them to our benefit. Oakley don't need to know anything about running the town, because I'll be in the background telling him what he has to do. And you, Jim, will have to take control of the mill and creamery operations now that Milt's no longer around, is why Oakley instead of you. This Mayor's job is just an honorary position, anyway, and after awhile, he'll be able to be insinuate himself into the Bishop's confidence, and we'll just take over from there."

"I don't know, Pa. It sounds pretty tricky to me. Are you sure Oakley can do it?"

"Well, that's why I picked him. He's young, don't know anything, and nobody will be suspicious of what he's doing. They'll just think he's got a lot to learn, and before you know it, we'll be sitting pretty. Ain't that right, Oakley?"

Oakley was thinking if he was elected Mayor, Hilaine would marry him for sure, and didn't give a darn about the job.

"It sounds like a mighty fine proposition, if you ask me," he replied.

But it was all for naught as it played out, with hardly anybody voting in favor of Oakley, who was still too young to vote.

There was a good snowstorm just before Thanksgiving that blanketed the mountains and the foothills in a foot or more of snow. Any traveling by wagon was converted to sleigh with the horses all bangled with bells that could be heard a half-mile or more before they made their appearance.

"It looks like we're going to have a snowy winter," the Bishop said to Roger Proudmire, who had brought his wife to town to get some flour, sugar, lard, etc.

"It piled up pretty deep for this time of year, and it feels like there's more on the way," Roger said, but he didn't want to carry on a long conversation with his mayoral adversary and head of the church. He was able to control his temper better since Colonel Wesford left town, but sometimes it was difficult, and talking to the Bishop was one of those times. He still held a grudge over the election, and thought the Bishop had cheated.

"I need a couple pair of wool socks and another metal bucket while the wife gets her goods together, Thorney."

"I'll grab the socks. You know where the buckets are back there. Just help yourself."

"What do you think the Henberry's were trying to accomplish putting Oakley in the race? If it wasn't for that, I might have won," Proudmire said.

"Well, you might've, and you know, now that everything is out in the open about Mrs. Bigknife and Milt, Henberry wants to take over the town. I think that's what it was," said Thorneycraft walking to the back of the store by Mr. Proudmire.

Mrs. Proudmire was over to the side looking at items that Mrs. Thorneycraft was displaying.

"We just got this in from the valley this week before the big storm. It's a new rack for canning stuff that you put in the water before you sterilize your bottles. They said using this saves time, 'cause all the bottles sit on the rack, and you can take them all out at once."

"Yes, yes. That'd be nice," said Mrs. Proudmire, "but I just wanted to buy some items for the kitchen, flour, sugar, etc. I don't have any room in my cupboards for something like that, and you know all this costs money."

"Your sister was just in and bought one. Said she had heard about it and just had to have it. She said she plans to..."

All talk ceased, and everybody in the store turned to gaze at the front door as it opened to see who the next customer was. The light was coming from behind, as he walked in, and his features were in the dark with his hat down low over his forehead obscuring his face even more, and the sheepskin collar of his coat was pulled up around his neck.

"I'll be right with you in just a minute," Mr. Thorneycraft said loud enough to carry the distance.

"Take your time there, Thorney. I'll just look around a bit," said the newcomer, pulling the coat collar down and turning his head to look at the candy.

"By golly, if it isn't Mr. Wesford! What brings you back to town? Here Roger, here's your socks," said Thorney, and practically threw them at Mr. Proudmire as he left to talk to his new customer.

The others followed him up front, not wanting to miss any news or gossip.

"It's a mighty cold day out there!" said Chappie, taking off his gloves, and stomping his boots on the floor to knock off some of the snow. He looked at the two women and raised a hand to his hat, then shook the hands of Thorney and Roger, greeting each in turn.

The salutations over with, Thorney asked again, "What brings you back to town, Chappie? I thought you had said your last goodbyes on the Fourth of July."

"As soon as I get warmed up, I'll tell you all about it. My face feels about froze off right now, but I don't want to get too close to the stove and burn myself up," he said and chuckled. "I been fighting the drifts since early this morning to make it up here today. Esther sends her greetings and told me to tell you have a nice Thanksgiving. She and Charlie and Milt are doing just fine. Milt came with me, but he's over at the Henberrys now."

"Cranky'll be glad to hear that Milt's back in town. Business has been kind of slow over there, according to him," said Thorney.

"Milt's now my deputy, and we're chasing some robbers that've been holding up about every place along the road. That's why we're up here, Thorney, to warn the town to be on the lookout for this gang. They're a bunch of hard cases and can't be trusted with anything of value. There's four of them in the gang, and they may be holed up somewhere in the Uintahs."

"If you need any help, Colonel, I'll be glad to pitch in rounding up these characters," said Roger.

"You'll do no such thing, Roger," said Bessie. "You got too many other things you have to do than go chasing a bunch of robbers."

"If we need volunteers, I'll let you know," Chappie said.

"I'll tell everybody that comes to church next Sunday," said the Bishop. "Are you looking for anything to buy today?"

"Nah, not yet, but I'll probably be needing some supplies before we go back down to the valley. Right now, I'll take a half-dozen pieces of that horehound candy in the case, if you don't mind, Thorney." Turning his attention to the Proudmires, he asked, "How's Brigham doing by now, Roger?"

"His leg didn't set right," said Bessie. "He still gets some pain at times and a slight limp, but he gets around fine. Freddy's still at our place helping with the pigs and stuff, though."

"Glad to hear that. How are your sister and family?"

They continued talking, bringing Chappie up on the news around town until he told them, "I got to be moving on to Cranky's place for a minute, but I'll see you again soon," knowing full well that he wouldn't be seeing them, at least not unless they should meet accidentally. Thorney had the candy ready, and Chappie handed him some change, but Mr. Proudmire said, "It's on me this time, Chappie."

He stepped back out into the cold air, untied Spottie's reins from the hitch rail, and walked through the snow to Cranky's saloon less than a quarter-mile away. The snow on the road was pretty well trampled down by horses and wagons, but the gutters were untouched. The walkway in front of the saloon had a few boot tracks leading to and from the door, too, with boot marks and horse's hooves at the hitch rail. But Chappie didn't tie his horse to the rail. Instead he put Spottie in the small stable next to Cranky's horses, unsaddled him, gave him some hay, and walked into the saloon.

Cranky was sitting at the table at the end of the bar drinking a cup of coffee. He glanced at the door as it opened and watched his next customer walk through it. He stood up when he recognized Chappie and said, "By golly, Chappie! Come in, come on in!" and shook his hand. "What can I get for you? Beer? Coffee?"

"Howdy, there, Cranky! I'll have a cup of coffee to warm me up, if you got any made, and you can catch me up on the happenings around here."

"How's the new family?" Cranky asked going through the door to his quarters to get the coffee.

"Esther's just fine, and Milt's visiting with his family right now. We're doing fine, yes sir, just fine," Wesford yelled at him.

"Do you think Milt'll be coming in here when he leaves the mill?" asked Cranky after he came back to the bar with two cups of coffee.

"He might. You worried that he might tear up the place again?"

"Well, heck, Chappie, you know how he is when he gets to drinking, and I just got all the chairs fixed from the last time."

"I don't think you'll have to worry about it. Milt's now on the side of the law, and that would cost him his job."

"What'd he do, get himself appointed a deputy sheriff or something?"

"Sort of," said Chappie, taking a sip of the coffee. "He's working for me as a Deputy Marshal, and we're on official business this time, Cranky, on the trail of a gang of robbers that held up the bank in Price not too long ago. Thought they might be headed this way. You haven't seen any strangers around have you in the last few days?"

"Not since it snowed. But you know how it is in the fall; we get a few hunters from the valley looking for deer around here."

"You don't suppose that I could stay here again for few days, do you? I'm going to be taking a look around and warning the folks about that gang of thieves."

"You can, but Esther's old house is still vacant. The old man that owned it died not long after you took her down to the valley. Old man Weaver, you remember him, don't you?"

"Oh, yeah. I remember those Utes were talking about him one night. He owned that house, too, huh? Esther never did say anything about it when we moved, other than she would take care of it, so we just moved out. What's going to be done with it?"

"I don't know. Maybe Weaver's brother will show up one of these days. It's a lot better accommodations there than here, though. You got your own stove, and there's even some wood that you left behind."

"I'll go over there later, then. About anything's better than this place, ha, ha, ha," Chappie chuckled. "How about another cup of this mud?"

"One more, and then I'll have to start charging you for it."

"I heard Oakley Henberry ran for Mayor. Did he get any votes?" Chappie asked when he received the cup of coffee.

"Not from me, he didn't, but one or two of his friends voted for him. He lost by a landslide, they said."

"He was too young to be running, anyway. I wonder what old man Henberry's got up his sleeve."

"Why don't you ask him, he's out there on his horse? Looks like he's headed home."

Chappie looked out the front window, but he had to walk to it to get a peek at Henberry going down the road. Through all the steam and dirt on the window, he wondered how Cranky recognized the man on the horse, but it was Henberry, all right. Chappie watched him ride past the store and had to open the door a crack to see him reach the corner and turn in the direction of the Six-Mile Road.

"Close the door, for crimany sakes!" yelled Cranky. "It's cold out there!"

"That was Henberry, but how did you know it through that dirty window?" Wesford asked, coming back to the bar.

"He's the only one that ever waves at me when he goes by, and I just got a glimpse of it."

"What was he doing in town?"

"Don't know, don't care."

"Don't he come in here anymore?"

"Don't have no reason to. He's only stopped in here twice since July. Even Young Jim and Oakley bin staying out of trouble, as far as I know. They haven't been in here much, either. When Milt left town, my business dropped off, and I been having to sell some of my pigs."

"He'll be surprised to see Milt, I bet," said Chappie, pushing his empty cup aside and standing up. "You sell your porkers in the fall, anyway, Cranky, so I'm reluctant to believe you did it for this place. I'm going to go take a look at Esther's house. You still got the key?"

"You bet. I got it in the back room, just a minute."

Chappie went to the front window and looked out while he was waiting for the barkeep to return. He wiped the steam from the window with his hand so he could see a little better. The sun was out shining brightly on the snow in the road, but there was no one moving around. He glanced toward the Bishop's store, where he could see a team pulling a sled toward the hitch rail, the driver pulling back hard on the reins. He didn't recognize him.

"Here's that key!" Cranky yelled from behind the bar. "Is somebody coming in?"

"Nah. There's somebody tying up at the store, though. I don't recognize him from here."

"Maybe he'll come over here later," Cranky was hoping for some business.

"I'm going to leave my horse in your stable for now. I'll come back and get him after I look at the house," Chappie said, leaving through the front door.

Wesford walked the nearly half-mile to his wife's former residence, making his way through the snow on the roadway. When he turned the corner to the creek, there were very few tracks in the snow. It looked like someone had ridden a horse up to the creek and back a couple of times. He followed the tracks as far as the house and turned in through the gate.

The late afternoon sun was hitting the house from the southwest as he entered on the darker east side. Walking through the front room, he was mainly interested in seeing what was still useable in the kitchen, since it was getting to be suppertime. The stove was still in good condition, so he went outside and got the last few pieces of wood still in the woodpile, came back and started a fire.

He went back to Cranky's stable while the stove was heating up, mounted his horse and returned to the house. The sun was setting, and it was turning colder, the snow crunching under his boots as he put the horse in the small corral and opened the barn door leading Spottie inside. Chappie unsaddled the horse, and took all his equipment and poke to the kitchen throwing it into a corner. He dug out some bacon and hardtack from a saddlebag, set them aside, then found his frying pan, sliced off some pieces of bacon, dropped them in and moved it to the stove.

Unrolling his blankets and arranging a bed near the wall by his saddlebags, he moved the bacon off the heat, retrieved his hardtack and sat down on the blankets to eat his meal. It was getting pretty dark in the room, so he dug out a candle from his saddlebags, lit it, set it up on the floor, and finished his supper sitting on his blankets with his back to the wall. The room was eerily quiet, only the crackling of the burning wood in the stove broke the silence. Chappie closed his eyes and leaned his head against the wall with his hat down over his eyes. He had almost dozed off when he heard the sound of crunching snow, barely noticeable. He quickly doused the candle light and laid down on the floor next to the wall. The crunching stopped when the light went out.

"Whoever's out there almost got a peek through the window," Chappie thought. "I'll just let him make the next move." He relaxed and let his body go limp, except for the hand on the pistol at his side, and listened intently for any noise outside.

The footsteps slowly retreated toward the front of the house, and then there were footsteps on the porch, followed by a loud knocking on the door.

"Open up, whoever's in there!"

Chappie slowly rose to a standing position and walked quietly to the door. He thought he recognized the voice, but he couldn't be sure.

Whoever it was, was getting anxious, "I know you're in there! Open up or I'm going to break the door down!" A fist crashed against the door, once, twice, three times, and the noise reverberated inside the room.

Chappie turned the door knob and flung open the door just as Mr. Fedderson was putting a shoulder into it. Fedderson's forward motion carried him almost across to the kitchen door.

"Come on in, Cal, why don't you! What's ..."

But Chappie didn't get his question finished, as Fedderson yelled, "Chappie! Chappie Wesford! What the heck're you doing in town?" and shook the hand that was put forward when he got himself arranged.

"Howdy, Cal! How's the wife and family?"

"Sorry to barge in on you like this, but I saw the light from the road as I was walking back home from the store, and I thought I better take a look. There hasn't been anyone in here since you left that I know of."

"No explanation necessary. I shouldn't have lit the candle, but it was getting dark. Are you all right? You sounded a little hoarse when you first yelled."

"No, no. I'm fine, just a slight cold, and Barbara and the family are fine, too. What're you doing here?"

Chappie explained his situation and asked Cal if he had seen any strangers in town the last few weeks.

"I was in Thorney's store just a day or two ago and there was a stranger came in and bought all the bacon and two 50-pound bags of flour, sugar, some salt, pepper, etc. He had a donkey with him that he loaded all his stuff on. Didn't think much of it, but I had to wait for Thorney to finish with him before I could get anything. He said he was getting supplies for deer hunting for him and his hunting partners. Never saw him before. He was a real rough-looking character, if you ask me. Even wore a six-shooter hanging low on his leg, not like a regular deer hunter from around here, although he had his rifle in the saddle holster. I don't know why he bought so much stuff, though. They must plan to stay out a long time."

"Didn't happen to mention his name, did he?"

"If he did, I didn't catch it."

Neither said anything for a minute and Fedderson asked, "Tomorrow is Thanksgiving and Barbara's cooking a big turkey tomorrow with all the trimmings, why don't you come eat with us?"

"Thanks a lot, Cal. I just might do that."

"What's Mrs. Wesford doing for Thanksgiving?"

"She'll be eating dinner with my mother and brother's family."

CHAPTER 11

Back in September, the elder James Henberry, when he heard the talk about Oakley being too young and not having a chance to become Mayor, sent a short letter to his younger brother, "Obie," short for Obadiah, the no-good of the family, and told him, "Bring a couple of your friends and come to Altaveel. I don't know exactly what you'll be doing, but by the time you get here, I'll have some work for you," he wrote.

And, of course, Obie and his friends showed up in town after robbing the bank in Price, and didn't say a word about it to Jim or his family. They avoided the town proper and went directly to the dairy barn at the bottom of the hill as the elder Henberry had instructed in the letter, arriving as the sun was setting. Mike and Eddie were there when they rode up, but soon left when Obie explained who they were, and since Mike had been forewarned by Mr. Henberry.

"We got to stash this money around here where nobody will accidentally run across it," said Obie, looking at the three companions who helped him steal it. "Any ideas?"

"We could just divide it up among us, and each one hides his own," the one called Bernie suggested. He was unshaven, scruffy, wearing a plaid wool coat over a couple of sweaters, and thought he was making a good suggestion.

"You should just hide it yourself, Obie. We all trust you since it was your idea to rob that bank and asked us to help you with it on the way here," Flood said. He was surprisingly clean-shaven, unlike the others, and the youngest of them. He didn't care about the money; he was just along for the action and excitement. Anytime he ran low on funds, he got in touch with his family back east, and a bank transfer was arranged. His family owned a furniture business, and it was busy shipping items west to meet the demand. Flood's clothes were new and in the latest fashions available in the woolen line. His family sent him west after a scrape where he managed to draw first and shoot another man, who he found out had been flirting with his girl. Ah, uncontrolled youth!

The other cowboy, Rye, said, "You can hide it, Obie, but just make sure I get my share when we split up."

"Well, that's two against one for me hiding it, so I'll just keep it all for now. You guys can hide out here tonight, while I go see what my brother wants us to do."

Obie mounted up and headed for the Henberry house, reached the grist mill in a few minutes and was knocking on the door in a short time.

The family was eating supper when he knocked.

"Go see who it is, Oakley," said the elder Henberry.

"Ma! Pa! It's Uncle Obadiah come to visit!" yelled Oakley from the front room.

"Well, bring him on in! Ma, set another plate on the table."

After they had eaten, the men moved to the front room and made themselves comfortable.

"That was a fine meal, Jim," said Obie. "I haven't ate a home-cooked supper for awhile. Yes, sir, a mighty fine meal."

"Glad you enjoyed it, but I didn't ask you to come here for the food. How many men did you bring with you?"

"Three."

"Good. Where are the others, now?"

"Up at the dairy barn like you told us. I told them to stay there for the night."

"Tomorrow, tell them to move up by the lake. The weather's turning bad, and it'll probably snow again pretty soon, but there's an old cabin in one of the side canyons they can stay in. I've furnished beds and some equipment for them. Then I want them to stay there and don't go wandering around. Tell them they're supposed to be on a hunting trip or something, if somebody should happen to come by."

"What do you want me to do?"

"Nothing right now, but you can help Jim and Oakley around the ranch and mill until I tell you. I've got big plans, and I don't want them ruined, so I'm taking it slow."

Over the next couple of days, young Jim and Oakley showed Obie the ranch and mill. There wasn't any grain coming in, so the mill was shut down until somebody needed flour and they loaded up their wagon with sacks of wheat and carted it to the Henberrys.

Oakley was still chasing Hilaine Fedderson every chance he got, and he was on his way home from the Feddersons after volunteering for ward teaching again when it started snowing and blowing. It was coming down hard and heavy, sideways from all the wind, making it difficult to keep his bearings, but once he got on Six-Mile Road, he let his horse take him home.

And when Oakley went outside in the morning, he had to wade through a foot-and-a-half-deep snow to the barn to check on the horse he had used last night.

"That was some storm we had," he said coming to the kitchen table from the barn to have breakfast. "There's about two feet of snow on the level. Good thing I left Fedderson's when I did, or I might not've got home last night."

"You better not've made a mess in the front room tracking in all that stuff," Mrs. Henberry warned.

"I was careful, Ma. Give me a couple of those pancakes before they're gone."

"You boys might take a ride up to the dairy barn and check on the milk cows this morning, and see if the milkers showed up," the elder Henberry said, stuffing a forkful of pancakes in his mouth. "They can't go too long without being milked."

"Do you want Uncle Obie to go along? He was still sleeping when I came down," the younger Jim said. "He don't appear too anxious to help out."

"I didn't ask him to come here to work on the ranch unless he wanted something to do, so he may not be too anxious to go to work for you boys," Mr. Henberry said.

"Why did you ask him to come here, Pa?" asked Oakley.

"I got a job for him and his friends."

And from the look he gave Oakley, no more questions were asked.

Obie made a trip to the cabin by the lake when he finally woke up. He wanted to check on his fellow bank robbers to ensure they were following directions. It took him a good four hours to go the twenty or so miles in the snow. Some of the drifts were deep, and he and his horse had to fight their way through in one stretch where the wind carried the snow and piled it up in a long drift. He found the cabin almost buried, the smoke from the chimney telling him its location.

Flood was outside digging a path through the snow with a shovel as Obie approached.

"Hey, there, Flood!" Obie yelled to give notice of his arrival.

Flood stopped shoveling and looked around, surprised to see anybody traveling in this weather, especially up here.

"Hi there, Obie!" he said, leaning on the shovel handle and watching Obie come through the snow.

"You fellers doing all right in this snow?" asked Obie when he had dismounted near Flood.

"As far as I know we are. I decided I'd clear a path to the horses to be doing something. I can only take so much of that gab in there. Did you get our money hid?"

"Let's go inside and I'll tell you all at once."

He tied his horse to a bush near the cleared trail, and they entered the cabin to find Rye sitting at the small table rolling a cigarette and Bernie lying on a cot covered with his blankets. Bernie sat up and pushed the covers off and sat on the side of the bed when he saw that Obie had come in.

"Well, Obie, when do we go to work?" Bernie asked. Rye remained silent staring at Obie and Flood.

"Not for awhile it looks like. Jim said he's working on a plan, but he wants us to hang around 'cause he'll need us when the action starts."

"This is a pretty boring place," said Bernie. "We got all that money and can't do anything with it. You hid the money, didn't you?"

"I got it stashed away, all right. Nobody's going to find it. I just came up to see if you needed any supplies or anything, and see what kind of layout this was. Do you need anything?"

"Nah, Bernie went to town and got some food, so we're set for now," Flood said.

"What'd you do that for, Bernie?" Obie said, with a steely stare. "I told you to stay low until I got back to you."

"We could've starved to death waiting for you, so I bought us some food."

"Next time you do anything dumb like that..... I told you to stay out of town and out of trouble. Did anybody see you come out this way?"

"Don't worry, Obie. I told the storekeeper I was buying stuff for my deer-hunting partners and left town in a different direction."

"Well, Jim told me to tell you you're all invited to Thanksgiving dinner at his house, tomorrow. Get yourselves cleaned up and presentable and come on down to the house in the afternoon."

"Where is this place?" asked Flood.

"Just west of the dairy barn. If you just follow this stream down the valley for about twenty miles, you'll find it. It's the only house around out there."

Obie hung around for another hour, talking with them about how they would spend the money after they finished this job and got their pay, and then he returned to his brother's house. Upon his arrival, he was surprised to see his nephew, Milt, there. He was sitting in the front room talking with young Jim.

"Howdy, Obie," said Milt. He had quit calling him "Uncle Obie" for some time. Obie just didn't seem like an uncle to him, and he hadn't seen him that much anyway.

"Milt. How you been?" Obie said, shaking Milt's hand. "Your Pa told me that you'd moved to the valley."

"Been down there a few months, and it's treating me right. Just here for Thanksgiving dinner. Ma makes the best turkey. What're you doing here in all this snow?"

"I brought a couple of friends out here this week to do some deer hunting up there in the mountains. Wasn't expecting it to snow so hard."

"Where're they? In town?"

"Nah. I took them up to that old hunting cabin by the lake, and told them they could stay there and use it as their headquarters. I just got back from there, and the snow's about buried the cabin, but they're all right. Just biding their time now for the snow to melt a little bit. They're coming down to eat turkey with us."

"Nice to see you again."

"Likewise."

"Well, Uncle Obie, you'll never guess what Milt's doing now," said Jim, having a difficult time containing himself.

"What *are* you doing, Milt?" asked Obie.

"He's a deputy U. S. Marshal!" announced Jim. "You're going to have to change your ways, or he'll haul you in!" he said and laughed heartily at his little joke.

"Ha-ha-ha-ha!" they all joined in the laughter, although Obie's was not a very hearty laugh.

"I didn't think a Henberry would ever be working on that side of the law," said Obie, "although we've always been law-abiding," he quickly added.

"I just took a job helping the Marshal, is all," said Milt.

"Cranky sure misses your business, Milt," Jim said. "Said he's losing money since you left town."

"I'll bet he is, but I've seen the error of my ways and don't drink hardly anything any more," he replied.

Oakley entered the room from outside, and hearing the remark said, "Maybe we ought to pay Cranky a visit tonight just for old time's sake."

"I wouldn't mind wetting my whistle, since I haven't had anything for awhile, and since Thanksgiving is tomorrow," said Obie.

"Maybe Pa'll come with us, then," said Oakley.

But the elder Henberry wasn't interested in going back to town. After supper the others saddled up and headed for a visit to Cranky's saloon. By the time they reached town, it was dark, and the store light was darkened as they went past. Oakley could see a light at the Fedderson place and knew that Hilaine would be home, but he thought better of paying a visit and entered the tavern with the others.

"Hey there, Cranky, set them up for the Henberrys!" Jim yelled walking to the bar.

Cranky was sitting at the table drinking coffee, but he looked up when the door opened. He immediately stood up and went behind the bar, grabbing a bottle of whiskey and some shot glasses, saying, "What'll it be tonight, fellers?"

"Give us a shot and a beer, and look who we got with us!" said Jim.

"Well, I'll be.....if it isn't Milt! How you been, Milt? This first one's on me, Milt, long time no see!"

"Howdy, Cranky! I see you got everything repaired from my last visit! I'll just have a cup of coffee, if you don't mind."

"By golly! Coffee coming up just for you! Who's this other feller with you?"

"This is our Uncle Obadiah Henberry, just visiting for Thanksgiving," said Oakley.

"Nice to meet you. What you going to drink, Obadiah?"

"I'll have a shot and a beer, too, if you don't mind."

They got settled in at a table next to the one where Cranky was drinking his coffee and began to talk among themselves when two Indians, Long Paul and Flat Paul, entered with the Greek George Lupadakis and went directly to the bar.

"Howdy, Cranky, and fellers," said Lupadakis. "Give me sonuvabit glass of wine, if you got, and dese fellers beer," pointing to the Indians.

"Your in town kind of late, ain't you, George?" asked Cranky.

"Bin working. Long Paul and Flat Paul halp repair sonuvabit barn. Dat sunovabit snow we got caused sonuvabit roof to fall in, sunovabit!" George replied with his favorite cuss word.

Cranky laughed. He was well used to Lupadakis' cussing. "I think that's the only cuss word he knows," he thought.

Obadiah was staring at the Utes as Cranky set a beer on the bar for each, and watched them take a drink. Standing up, he threw his empty beer glass at the wall across the saloon. It crashed into the only picture in the place, another painting by Eddie Jensen of a mountain scene with a deer, or was it an elk, nobody could tell for sure, standing in a clearing looking at a fawn near the edge of the forest, and the glass broke into a thousand pieces, smashing a hole through the canvas before the remnants fell to the floor.

The sudden movements and noise caused George and the Utes to turn around and see what was going on. Everybody at the Henberry table was on their feet waiting to see what was coming next.

Obadiah, still standing and staring at the Utes then Cranky, said, "If I knew you'd been serving Injuns in here, I wouldn't've come in! I don't drink with no Injuns!" But he didn't make an attempt to leave.

George was the first to speak next, "Sonuvabit! Dese my sonuvabit frens! We drink alla time together. Sonuvabit!" looking at Obie with a strange stare.

Jim, Oakley and Milt knew Lupadakis and thought his cussing was funny, too, but Obie took exception to being called a sunovabit; at least, he thought he was being called that.

"Nobody calls me a son of a..... without suffering consequences!" and started to pull his gun.

Milt grabbed his wrist before he could get it out of the holster, and said, "You don't want to do that, Obie. George is unarmed, and those Indians are well known around here and come in here all the time. They help Cranky take care of the place."

"I still ain't drinking with no Injuns, and what's that guy calling me a son of a..... for anyway."

"That's just George, he calls everybody that, don't you George?" said Oakley.

"Sonuvabit yas! Ever'body is sonuvabit, you bet, frens and en'mies, too. But I still drink wit' muh sonuvabit Injun frens, you bet, I do. No sonuvabit stop me, no sir. Sonuvabit!"

"There! He did it again, called me a son of a ...!" yelled Obadiah, but Milt still had his wrist in his grip, and all he could do was stare at Lupadakis.

The front door opened again, and in came the Bishop and Fedderson, and straight to the bar they went.

Cranky greeted them with, "Good evening, Bishop. Nice to see you on Thanksgiving eve. What brings you and Cal out tonight, and what can I serve you?"

Not realizing they had interrupted the beginning of a brawl, but seeing everyone on their feet, the Bishop said, "Be seated, gentlemen. Cal and I have been making a few house calls to spread the Word of God on this Thanksgiving eve and offer comfort and sustenance to those who may need it, huh, Cal? I'll have a sarsaparilla, Cranky. Would you gentlemen be interested in hearing our message tonight?" he asked looking at the Henberrys, and noticing Milt still holding Obie's wrist, added, "Who's that you're holding on to, Milt? Nice to see you again? You're not getting in trouble again are you?"

"Evening Bishop," he replied, letting go of the wrist. "No, no, staying out of trouble. Obie, here, was just trying to grab Oakley's drink. This is Uncle Obadiah Henberry, Pa's brother from southern Utah thereabouts. Obie, this is Bishop Thorneycraft and Cal Fedderson from the church."

Obadiah gave Milt a funny look and said, "Evening, Bishop, Cal." He stared at the Utes, who were not paying any attention, but sipping their beers.

"Nice to meet another of the Henberry clan," said Cal. He looked at Cranky and said, "I'll have a sarsaparilla, too, Cranky, before Thorney drinks it all. How's Long Paul and Flat Paul this evening?" he asked the Utes.

"Him no like Utes," Long John said, staring at Obadiah. "He try start trouble with George, friend of Utes, but Milt stop him."

George put his glass down when he heard his name, "'Alo, Thorney, you try make me Mormon tonight, huh?" he said, as if nothing had gone on earlier.

"Ha-ha-ha!" Thorney laughed at the remark. "Not tonight, George. We didn't even know you were in town."

"Well, what's your message tonight?" asked Jim.

"Let us have a drink to celebrate the Lord's works here on earth in honor of Thanksgiving tomorrow," said Cal.

"I ain't drinking with no stinking Injuns!" said Obie. "Let's get out of here, Jim!" And he stomped out the door in a huff.

"Come on, Oakley, Milt. We better get on home," said Jim. "Sorry we can't listen to your preaching tonight, Bishop. Goodnight." And he and Oakley left, with Milt telling them he'd catch up with them in a few minutes.

"Good riddance to sonuvabit," said George. "Give us 'nudder, Cranky, sonuvabit."

"I guess we can't leave any message here tonight, Cal. We may as well go on home," said Thorney.

"How come you didn't go with them, Milt?" asked Cal.

"I want to talk with Cranky a minute in private, to see if I owe him any money."

"Let's go in back where we can parley private," said Cranky, leading the way.

"See you in church, George," Cal said as he and Thorney left.

"Dem sonuvabit try get me come their sonuvabit church alla sonuvabit time," said George to the Utes.

"That Fedderson good man," said Long Paul.

"Him good," agreed Flat Paul.

"Sonuvabit," agreed George.

CHAPTER 12

Chappie climbed out of his bedroll on the floor, stretched, then sat down on the blankets and pulled his boots on, got up again and walked into the kitchen. There, he broke the ice on the wash basin, washed his face in the cold water, dried off with a dirty shirt he had dug out of a saddlebag last night, and made a fire in the stove to heat up the left over coffee. He went outside and checked on Spottie and looked around for some more wood he could burn.

There was nobody stirring in the town that he could see, although there was smoke coming from the Fedderson chimney and some more from other houses behind the store on the south side of town. Cranky's place was closed for the day. He walked through the snow to the woodshed by Cranky's stable and loaded up his arms with wood, brought it back to the rear of Esther's old house, and dropped it by the door, thinking, "I should've done this last night."

He carried some into the house and put it by the stove, then poured a cup of coffee and walked to the window, looked around, observing the schoolhouse and the field behind it. He could see where the creek ran to the north by the few willows along the bank and wondered why there weren't any trees growing there. "Maybe they cut them down early on for lumber or firewood," Chappie said to himself.

Not seeing much but the snow-covered ground and the school, he turned around and went back to the kitchen and moved his fry pan over the heat after dropping a piece of dried meat into the grease. Chappie found some hardtack in a saddle bag and stood in front of the stove waiting for the meat to get ready. Before he took the meat from the pan, he cut it in smaller pieces so he could eat it on his hardtack. He went back to his bed, sat down with his back against the wall and was enjoying his primitive breakfast. He was almost finished when he heard voices outside the window. He took a peek with his head barely above the sill, and was staring into the eyes of Long Paul on the other side of the pane with both hands around his face trying to see in. Long Paul, startled, jumped back and bumped into Flat Paul, who was trying to look over his shoulder. They both almost fell down as Chappie yelled, "Long Paul! Come on in! You and Flat Paul!"

Thinking they had seen a ghost, they turned around and started to run away. Chappie raised the window and yelled again, "Hey, Long Paul, it's me, Chappie Wesford, come on back. I want to talk to you!"

Long Paul stopped, but Flat Paul kept running up the road toward the town lifting his legs high to get through the snow. Long Paul slowly came back to the house and went to the front door, which was open now with Chappie standing in it waiting for him to return.

"It's only me, Long Paul."

"I think you're ghost, Chappie. What you do here in ole Weaver's place?"

"Just visiting. Do you think your brother will come back?"

"Flat Paul come back pretty soon."

"Well, tell me, have you seen any strangers around here lately. The law's looking for some bank robbers that may have come through here not too long ago."

"Me no remember very good," Long Paul answered, holding out a hand.

"You better tell me or I'll haul you in for drinking. I don't pay for information," said Chappie with a steely glare.

Long Paul took a better look at the lawman, then dropped his hand, and said, "Me no see too much, but one day see man leave store and ride that way," pointing to the east. "Never see before. He ride horse and pull burro behind."

"Did you get a good look at him? Would you know him, if you saw him again?"

Flat Paul came panting up to the open door with a terrified look on his face, until Long Paul told him, "Talk to Chappie. Tell him 'bout stranger."

"Ai-i-i, Chappie! I think you ghost, so run away."

"What about that stranger you saw, Flat Paul. What was he doing in town?"

"Him buy big load in store. Have hard time loading mule. I watch him."

"Did you see him leave town, too?"

"He leave that way," pointing east.

"Do you know why he bought so many supplies?"

"Nope. Maybe he have friends in mountains."

"Would you know him, if you see him again?"

"Maybe."

"Well, thanks Long Paul, Flat Paul. Cranky been treating you right?"

"You bet. Him good man," said Flat Paul.

"What're you doing in town today? It's a holiday for everybody. You going to Thanksgiving dinner with the Bishop?" Chappie asked with a smile.

"Ha-ha-ha! That funny!" said Long Paul. "Oh, another stranger we see last night at Cranky's. They call him Obie, Oba...di... or something. Him uncle of young Henberrys. He no like Indians, no drink with us. Almost had trouble, but Bishop and Fedderson came in saloon, and he and Henberrys leave."

"He wasn't the one loading up the mule, was he?"

"Nah. Never see that one again."

"Where you going?"

"We go chop wood for Cranky."

"Can you bring me some, and I'll pay good money for it?"

"All right. We make nice woodpile for you, two dollars."

"What? That's robbery! Too much!"

"We even fill up wood box in house, two dollars."

"How about one dollar? And just make a nice pile out there?" Chappie said, pointing.

"Hm-m, all right, one dollar," said Long John.

Chappie gave Long John a dollar against his better judgment and hoped that they would do what they said.

"See you boys later," he said.

Chappie went to the stable and saddled up Spottie, mounted and rode out of town, headed for the Six-Mile Road. He thought he'd better pay a visit to the Henberrys.

He took a gander around the mill, when he reached the Henberry set-up, but no one was working today, as he figured. Knocking on the front door of the house, Mrs. Henberry opened it.

"Well, my gosh, if it isn't Mr. Wesford. Happy Thanksgiving! Come in, come in!"

"Howdy, Mrs. Henberry. How are you and the family? I just came out to see Milt, if he's here. Thought I'd get..." but he was interrupted by the elder Jim.

"By golly, Colonel Wesford has come to see us on Thanksgiving! What're you doing roaming around in the snow, anyway?"

"Howdy, Jim! Happy Thanksgiving to you! Just came by to parley with Milt," he said, shaking hands with Mr. Henberry. "Is he home?"

"Hey, Milt! Chappie wants to talk with you! Come down here!" yelled Henberry. "Go see where he is, will you?" he said to his wife.

"Everything going good for you, Jim?" Chappie asked while waiting for Milt.

"Right as rain, yes sir, just fine, just fine. Yourself?"

"Can't complain. That was a good storm we had, wasn't it?"

"It was. Did you get any snow down in the valley?"

"Oh, yes, a goodly amount. Good for the crops next year. We always...," Chappie saw Milt enter the room and didn't end his sentence.

"Hi, there, Chappie. Got some news? Let's go out to the barn. I want to show you that hoof. I think it's healing up real good," Milt said.

"See you later, Jim," said Chappie.

"Ain't you staying for Thanksgiving dinner?"

"Thanks, but I been invited to the Feddersons."

"Oh, well, see you later, then."

Out in the barn, Milt lifted his horse's hind leg so they could get a look at the bottom of the hoof.

"It looks like it's healing up pretty good now. He'll be ready to ride in a day or two. Did you get a lead on the bank robbers, Chappie?"

"I don't know for sure. Three people so far have told me about a stranger in town buying up all the supplies he could load onto a mule and heading out of town to the east. But nobody knew where he was going, except he was getting some supplies for a party of deer hunters. He could be getting them for the thieves, too. What about yourself? Anything going on around the mill or the dairy?"

"Well, my so-called Uncle Obadiah showed up, saying that my father had asked him to come here, and he brought along three buddies. They're coming to dinner today. Maybe I can learn more about them."

"All right. See what you can find out, and I'll be talking with you tomorrow or so. I guess I better get on into town before they eat all the turkey."

They went back to the front of the house, and Chappie climbed on Spottie, waved goodbye to Milt, then rode back up the Six-Mile Road. Turning on the main road through town, he gave the place a once-over, looking at the scattered buildings as Spottie took him past. The storefront needed new paint. "The Bishop's letting things get run down," he said to himself. "And Cranky's place don't look too good either, but it never did have paint. And Weaver's old house is ready to fall any day, it looks like." He could hear the sound of an axe biting into wood, and figured it was the two Utes still chopping firewood for himself and Cranky.

He went past the old schoolhouse and arrived at the Fedderson place, where he tied Spottie's reins to the new, wooden hitch rail, thinking, "Cal must not have enough to do. He doesn't need a hitch rail when there's some trees and bushes nearby." Chappie knocked on the front door, and it was opened by Hilaine.

"Come on in, Mister Wesford, I hope you're hungry, 'cause we got a lot to eat!"

"Howdy, Hilaine! I've brought along a big hunger, all right. I'm so hungry I could eat the saddle off a horse, right now," he replied with a laugh.

"Pa's out in the chicken coop again, but he won't be long, and Ma's in the kitchen getting everything ready with the help of Darlena and Freddy. We'll go in there and see if we can help."

And not giving him a chance to answer, she turned and headed for the kitchen.

"Here's Colonel Wesford, Ma! He's going to help us set the table."

And in came Cal and his oldest son, Max, Cal saying, "Make yourself at home, Chappie, I think we're about ready to eat. At least, I am! Everyone take a seat and we'll talk later! Chappie, you can sit there, next to Hilaine, if you don't mind."

Everybody but Mrs. Fedderson and Darlena took their seats, and waited for the turkey to be put on the table. Darlena brought in a large dish of dressing, then potatoes and gravy, followed by vegetables and sweet potatoes. The turkey was put on last in a large platter by Mrs. Fedderson, after which she took the chair next to Cal, and Darlena sat between Max and Freddy.

"Max, your turn to give the blessing," said Cal.

"Our Father in Heaven, we thank Thee for the many blessings we have received during the year and thank Thee for our good health and all the food on the table for this Thanksgiving dinner. .... Oh, Lord, we ask thee to bless this family, that we may continue living our lives in peace and prosperity, and ask that our guest today be blessed with good fortune and success and that his family also be found in good spirits upon his return. We ask thee to bless this food that it may nourish and strengthen our bodies and satisfy the hunger pangs. We ask these blessings in the name of the Father, the Son and the Holy Ghost, amen."

Everyone commenced digging into the food, saying how good it was.

"Delicious, that turkey, ah-h, cooked just right, Ma," Helaine said.

"Pass me some of them taters and gravy, and sweet taters, to go with it," said Freddy.

"How you been anyway, Barbara, and how's your sister?" asked Chappie, swallowing some of the turkey.

"I've been fine, Mr. Wesford, and Bessie's been doing good, too. How's your new wife, Esther, getting along down there?" she replied. "The Relief Society sure misses her. They didn't realize how much sewing she did for them."

"She's fine, met some nice people there and is helping out the church, too. Settled in pretty well. Mm-mm. This is sure good, Barbara."

"Darlena cooked the potatoes and whipped together the dressing. She's going to make some man a good wife," said Barbara.

"It's all good!" said Freddy. "I can't wait for the pumpkin pie! I'm about ready, Ma!"

"You still working for the Proudmires, Freddy? And you, Max, still working at the dairy?" asked Chappie.

They both answered in the affirmative.

"You still thinking about leaving home, Freddy?"

"Yes, sir, I am, as soon as I get enough money saved up. I should have enough by next summer."

"We've decided to help him out a little bit and let him go chase his dreams," Mr. Fedderson said.

"It's against my better judgment, but he's got his heart set on learning about trains and engines and such," said Barbara.

"It'll be good for him. He'll learn a lot. There ain't no schools like that around here. I wish him good luck," said Chappie. "Is Oakley still romancing you, Hilaine?"

"Oh, yes, he comes by whenever he gets the chance," she replied.

"Seems like it's about every day," Cal said.

Max had to put his two cents in, "He's like a love-sick dog these days," and laughed.

"You're just jealous, 'cause you don't have no girlfriend," Darlena said.

"Ha-ha-ha! That'll be the day!"

And the afternoon passed pleasantly by with lots of joking and conversation about everything families talk about. The males had to go outside after the meal to check on the animals. Max and Freddy milked the cows, while Cal and Chappie talked about everything under the sun they could think of except the reason Chappie was in town.

It was well after dark when Chappie left.

The next day Milt rode into town with Oakley and Jim. Jim had a long list of supplies to order from the store, and Oakley came in to visit with the Feddersons, while Milt wanted to talk with Wesford. Oakley and Milt went into Cranky's to see if anyone else was there.

"How was Thanksgiving, Cranky?" asked Milt.

"I feel like a stuffed pig, I ate so much," he replied.

"Are you going to have a beer Oakley? I'll have a glass," said Milt.

"Nah. I reckon I'll go see if Hilaine's home. Got to talk to her about something important," Oakley reckoned, after seeing nobody else was in the saloon.

Cranky drew a glass of beer and put it in front of Milt on the bar.

"Where's that Obie feller this morning?"

"I guess he's at home. He wasn't up when we left."

"He's not a very likeable sort to my mind. Wouldn't even drink with those Utes here," said Cranky.

"I've never had much to do with him, even though he's supposed to be an uncle. Just never cared for him that much, and he hasn't been around in years. Have you seen Chappie around?"

"Oh, yeah. He's staying in Esther's old house. He stopped here the other night and wanted to stay here again, but I suggested that place, and I guess that's where he is. You fellers got a lead on those robbers you're looking for?"

"Don't know," said Milt, taking a sip of his beer. "This stuff don't taste good anymore, since I stopped drinking."

Cranky chuckled and said, "What'd you order it for, if you didn't want it?"

"Well, don't worry. I'll pay you for it."

"If you ain't going to drink it, you don't have to pay for it this time."

"I'm going to drink it. I just said it doesn't taste good, was all."

Cranky was getting ready to argue some more with him, but the back door opened and Chappie walked in and took a seat at the bar by Milt.

"The way things are up here, I might as well move my office to Altveel. It seems everything that comes up, this town is involved in some way," he said. "If we don't get a break pretty soon, I'm heading back to the valley, though."

"What is the matter, getting homesick already?" asked Milt.

"Give me a sarsaparilla, Cranky, and then Milt and I are going to take a little walk."

They were leaving by the back door, when Henry Dugan entered the front, saw them, and yelled, "Hey, Colonel Wesford! Can I talk to you a minute?"

Chappie and Milt came back to the bar to see who was yelling at them.

"I'm Henry Dugan, Marshal. We met in here one night in June or July, the last time you came to Altveel. I got to talk to somebody about my mule, and there ain't no law around here."

"Well, Henry, I don't know whether I can help you out or not. I don't usually get involved in local jurisdictions, but we'll listen to your story, and maybe offer a suggestion. Let's sit down and have a drink," Chappie said.

"Thanks, I got to tell somebody. I'll have a beer, Cranky. Howdy, Milt. Nice to see you again. Darn it, Marshal! My best mule, Ole Butter, was stolen," began Henry.

Cranky set up the beer for Henry without saying anything, which was unusual for him, but he wanted to hear the details maybe even more than the two lawmen so he could spread the news among his customers.

"It happened a few days afore the big snowstorm. You know I own a ranch out to the southwest a ways, and just afore the storm, Ole Butter came up missing. Some dirty, cowardly thief snuck into my barn and took Ole Butter right out of there. I had him locked in the barn 'cause I could tell that a storm was on the way, and they just took him right out of there without even a how-do-you-do. Cowardly bas---uh--thieves," an agitated Henry said.

"Now, Henry, just relax. No need to get all upset. Like I said, I can't probably give you any help, since it's a local matter, but did you see them take him or hear anything unusual the night of the theft, or anything else that would help the law?" asked Chappie.

"Didn't hear nary a thing! Right in the middle of the night, they stole him. My wife never heard a thing, neither. She would be the one to hear something, if there was any noise or anything like that. Got good ears, she has, but neither one of us heard a thing, Marshal."

"What color was he, Ole Butter?"

"Just the standard mule color, dark grayish brown, I would say."

"Did he have any distinguishing marks or something that would make him a little different than the other animals?"

Henry drained his glass, sat it on the bar, and said to Cranky, "Fill it up again, Cranky."

"I was just thinking about that, but I can't think of anything remarkable other than his disposition. I named him Ole Butter because he had the easiest disposition of any mule I ever saw." Henry took a swallow of the full glass, and continued, "He was the easiest mule to work with, would do anything you asked him, he would."

"Well, Henry, about all we can do is report this to the County Sheriff and keep our eyes open for him, wouldn't you say, Milt?"

"That's all we can do, all right," said Milt. "We'll keep our eyes open for Ole Butter."

"Leastways, then, I won't have to make a trip down there in this weather, if you turn in a report on it, will I?"

"Nope, you shouldn't have to. We were just leaving. Come on, Milt, let's go before we hear from somebody else."

They left through the back door and were about halfway to Chappie's house before either spoke.

"Are you thinking what I'm thinking?" Chappie asked. "Ole Butter was the mule the Utes saw in town being loaded up. I'll lay you odds on that."

"Yeah, I'll bet it was, too."

"You know those fellers that came to dinner, Obadiah's partners, they're roosting up at the lake where you caught Oakley and me that day. There's a cabin up there in a side canyon we put together for when we went deer hunting. Pa didn't want them hanging around the house or mill."

"Did they look anything like that description we got for the bank robbers?"

"Some. But it's hard to tell for sure. One of them said he'd been to town to buy some bacon, but Obie shut him up before he could go any further. Obie seems to be the leader. They sure hung around him, trying to get him alone for some reason. I wouldn't be surprised if they robbed that bank, and I wouldn't put past Uncle Obie to be the one behind it. He's done time for trying to steal money before."

"We don't have any evidence of anything yet. Just keep your eyes on Obie. Sooner or later they got to get together with that money, if they're the ones who have it. I think I'll take a ride up to the lake and have a look around."

"You're going to have to be careful. They're not just farmers out hunting deer," Milt warned.

"I know, I know. You want a cup of coffee?" Chappie asked when they reached the house.

"Nah."

"I've got a couple more questions to ask you about your Uncle Obie, but I want some coffee. Let's go inside, and I'll heat up my leftovers. I don't particularly like that coffee over at Cranky's."

Sitting at the table drinking the coffee, Chappie said, "How often does Obie visit the family?"

"That's only the fourth or fifth time I've seen him. He lives down south somewhere, since he got out of prison. I don't know why he's here now, other than Pa asked him to come for some reason. I think he feels sorry for him, and has lined up a job of some kind for him."

"What's he do down south?"

"I think he owns a small farm, but I wouldn't swear to it. He's the black sheep of the family according to Pa, a never-do-well, Pa calls him, but he's still my brother, he says."

"Sounds to me like he sort of fits the description of that one feller the teller was talking about at the bank. We got to keep our eyes on him and those others, too. I hope your Pa ain't planning anything criminal."

"Whatever he's got planned, it'll be entirely within the law. He don't need to do anything to get more money. He and Ma get enough from the mill and dairy."

"Maybe we both ought to ride up to the lake and see if they got Henry's mule. Maybe we can hold them on that, if they do, at least one of them."

"All right."

"Their tracks are easy to follow around here in this snow," Milt said, when they arrived in the vicinity of the small lake.

"Why don't you go on to the cabin, and I'll circle around and see if I can spot that mule. I'll come on in, if I see it. Just keep them occupied for awhile."

Chappie rode his horse through the brush concealing himself the best he could until he thought he better proceed on foot. Tying Spottie to a tree, he walked up the side of the mountain behind which the cabin stood, taking a good look around from his high viewpoint. He spotted the animals in a small corral about thirty yards behind the cabin. Only two horses were out in the open, the rest presumed to be in the ramshackle barn, which was put together using the steep mountainside as the rear wall. He diligently proceed to walk down the incline, making as little disturbance as possible, and climbed down next to one sidewall, where he found a crack he could take a peek through. With the cracks letting in enough light, he spotted the mule tied up to a 6"x6" roof support.

He retreated over the mountain back to Spottie, climbed on the horse, and rode right up to the cabin door. Staying astride his horse, he yelled, "Milt, are you in there?" knowing full well he was.

The door opened, and Milt and Rye were both standing in the opening.

"Howdy, Marshal! What brings you up this way?" said Milt.

"I heard you were up here with your Uncle's friends, and I needed to talk to you. Who are those fellers with you?"

"They're Obie's partners. This feller is called Rye; the two others are Bernie and Flood. I'd like you to meet Marshal Wesford, boys. You might as well get down and come on in and be sociable."

"What're those other two doing in there?"

Milt stepped out of the doorway and to the side closer to Chappie. "I don't think they like lawmen too much."

"Well, Rye, since you seem to be the more sociable, I'd like to ask you a question and maybe you are one of those other fellers can answer it. A rancher named Henry Dugan reported that his mule was stolen the other night. Have you seen any mules wandering around up here?"

Rye relaxed against the doorframe, looked around behind him, then answered, "Don't reckon we have, Marshal, but you're welcome to take a look around. Right, Bernie?"

"Suppose so. We don't have nothing to hide," Bernie answered from the cot he was sitting on.

"Just a minute, there! Ain't you supposed to have some kind of warrant or something before you go searching a feller's property?" said Flood, who had come to the doorway.

"Well, I just asked you a question 'bout a missing mule, and this feller, Rye, said you hadn't seen it, but when's the last time you took a look in your barn? I spotted a mule in there that fits the description of Mr. Dugan's Ole Butter. Any idea how it got in your barn?"

"Nary a one," Bernie yelled, and then proceeded to say, "He must've just wandered in there to get out of the snow and cold."

"If he did, he tied himself up to a post, too! I'll ask you again, which one, or did all of you steal him from Dugan's barn before the snowstorm? And which one took him to town to carry your supplies up here?"

"I did!" Bernie yelled. "But I didn't steal him from no barn. That was Obie's idea, and I ain't going to take any rap of his."

"Milt, why don't you go get Ole Butter and bring him on out here. We'll take him back to town and Dugan can pick him when he has a chance."

But Rye had other ideas, "Just a minute there, Milt! Nobody's going to take that mule anywhere!"

Rye pulled his gun and was aiming at Milt, and the Marshal shot him in the arm.

"Don't anybody in there get any ideas!" Chappie yelled, "Come on out here with your hands in the air!"

Rye was knocked back into the room with the blast, dropping his gun, and let out a yell, "Aaa-r-gh! My arm!"

He bumped into Flood, who was trying to draw his pistol, but the gun was knocked out of his hand and went flying into the room.

Milt jumped through the doorway with gun drawn to find Bernie still sitting on the cot, scratching an armpit.

Chappie jumped off his horse and followed Milt, covering Rye and Flood.

"All right! Outside! Everybody outside!" Chappie said. "Milt, take that rope off Spottie and start tying up Rye and Flood while I keep them covered. We'll take them to town and hold them 'til we get to the bottom of this mule theft. Rye, I'm charging you with interfering with the law in the course of its duties, and Flood you'll face similar charges. Bernie didn't do anything yet, so he's still a free man for now. Take them to the corral and tie them to a post while we saddle their horses. Bernie you can get their saddles and bridles and start getting the horses ready."

"I didn't interfere with no law," said Rye. "I was just going to stop Milt from getting our mule. He ain't no lawman. And fix up my arm before I bleed to death. It hurts powerful."

"You might as well show him your badge, Milt. Milt's a Deputy Marshal."

When they were ready to travel, they left Bernie sitting on his cot with the warning not to be stupid and try to help his partners escape, and took Rye, Flood and the mule to the house where Chappie was staying. It was after dark when they reached the house and tied up the two prisoners back-to-back sitting on the floor in the bedroom.

CHAPTER 13

Milt went on home after he left Wesford with the two prisoners. His Uncle Obie was still up and had gone down to the kitchen for a glass of water when he heard him come in. Obie asked, "Out kind of late tonight, huh?"

"Yup. Been looking for a mule. Henry Dugan's mule was stolen and we been out looking for it."

"Have any luck?"

"Yup. Caught a couple of polecats, too. Friends of yours. Rye and Flood."

"They didn't steal no mule, did they?"

"Don't know, but they were interfering with the law, and Rye got shot in the arm. Look, I'm tired and am going to bed. Bernie will tell you all about it when you see him."

Obie was up before anyone else and left to go see Bernie.

Bernie was on his way to talk to Obie, too, and they met on Six-Mile Road.

"What the heck happened yesterday, Bernie? I hear Rye got shot and Flood's in trouble. What went on?"

"Did you know that Milt's a Deputy Marshal?"

"I heard it, yep, but I don't believe it. He drinks too much to be on the side of the law, according to his Pa."

"He sure helped the Marshal haul in Rye and Flood, and they took the mule you stole with them. Rye was stupid. They were just looking around for the mule, and Rye pulled his gun to keep them out of the barn. That's when the Marshal shot him, and Flood was going to help Rye, but got his gun knocked out of his hand. Nothing that I could do, because they had us covered. They tied them up and brought them into town and put them in a house. I followed them and stayed around and slept a little bit in the barn behind it."

"What do you think is going to happen to them? If they start talking about the bank money, the Marshal will know we robbed that bank. I think we ought to make plans to take the money and head for other parts. What do you think we ought to do?"

"It don't look too good for us. I think we should leave with the money and let them take their chances with the law. And no waiting around."

"I got to go back to my brother's place and get the money and I'll meet you on this road, again this afternoon. I got to think of a reason to tell my brother why I'm leaving that sounds good. Bring everything in the cabin that you can load on your horse and put anything left over in the barn there. We'll make do without it. Does that sound all right with you?"

"What about Rye and Flood? We going to leave them here?"

"We have to. If they don't say anything about the robbery, they might get off easy and can catch up with us. If they tell the law about it, they'll be in prison for a long time."

"Well, I'm ready to leave right now, but I better go clean up the cabin. I ain't going to lose my part of that money after all this. With all this snow, it's going to take me awhile to get up there and back or my horse is going to be wore out."

"It's still early, just barely daylight, and I don't want to seem in a big hurry to leave my brother's place, so I won't get back here until just before sundown. That should give you plenty of time, and you might even have to wait for me awhile. And we'll split the money up right here and hightail on out of here in different directions."

"All I want is that money, and I'm going to Kansas or Texas or someplace, maybe even Wyoming."

"I'll see you this afternoon," Obie said, and turned his horse around and went back to the Henberry house.

Meanwhile, Chappie made some coffee after he got some sleep, and pondered his next move. He looked at the prisoners still sleeping back to back on the hard floor, and thought, "Must be awful tired." He went over and jabbed Flood with the toe of his boot.

"Time to wake up, gentlemen! Got a cup of coffee ready for you. Here, let me give you a hand to sit up."

Rye moaned in pain, as Chappie grabbed him under the arms and sat him upright. "Maybe I can find a doctor to tend to you today, if you're nice and cooperative. And maybe I'll ask the Utes to give me some help while you're staying here."

"How about untying us? My hands feel like their going to fall off, "said Flood.

"I'm going to loosen the ropes a bit, so you can drink your coffee, and eat some bread and bacon. How would that be?" asked Chappie. "But, first, you got to tell me about that mule. How come you had him in your barn?"

"Obie said we'd need him to carry supplies, and he was right. He took him out of the barn. Neither one of us had anything to do with that," said Rye with a grimace.

"What were you fellers running from?"

"We weren't running from anything just that Obie had to go see his family first, before we could do any deer hunting. He showed us that cabin and told us to wait for him," Rye said.

"Who's got the money?"

"What money? We don't know what you're talking about, Marshal," said Flood.

"Are your arms getting sore, yet, starting to lose feeling in the hands? Maybe if you're honest with me, those ropes could be loosened a little more or maybe even untied. I been following you all the way from Price after the bank robbery there. What'd you do with the money?"

"Tell him, Flood, maybe he'll get me a doctor," Rye said.

"Tell him what?"

"That we were just getting ready for a good deer hunt is all. Maybe if you untie my hands I'll tell you all about it, Marshal. I can't feel anything," said Rye.

This palaver went on for quite awhile, until Chappie loosened the ropes and let them drink some coffee, eat some bread and bacon. He then tightened the rope again and wrapped the long end around a stove leg and secured it. If they got to their feet, they couldn't get out the door without untying the rope, which would be virtually impossible. He told them, "If you're lucky enough to get this untied, I won't come chasing after you until I catch up with the rest of the robber gang." He went out the door.

"Hey, Cranky," he said going into the saloon. "Draw me a beer and tell me what's new in town."

"Sit down at the table at the end of the bar, and I'll have one with you."

"Have you seen a feller named Obadiah Henberry lately?"

"He was in here the other night causing trouble with the Utes," said Cranky, drinking some of the beer out of the glass. "Jim and Oakley were with him and Milt. He's a bad hombre, you ask me."

"Milt was telling me about that," said Chappie, taking a sip of his beer. "Why do you think old Jim asked him to pay him a visit? Any ideas?"

"I think he would like to take over everything around. He wants more power. That's why Oakley ran for mayor to get more influence, is my guess."

"Some people just never have enough, do they. I guess he was going to use Obie and his partners to run some of it after he gets his hands on whatever he plans to get. But I think that gang stole that bank money on the way here, and if he hadn't stole Henry's mule, I'd never know the difference." And he took a couple more sips of his beer, the last a good swallow.

"He stole that mule? That was a pretty dumb thing to do, wouldn't you say?"

"Not very bright. If Henry Dugan comes in, you can tell him his mule is in your stable. I put it there last night. I'm surprised you didn't hear me."

"Who was that feller pulling him around town?"

"I think his name is Bernie."

"Never heard of him before," Cranky said, and took another swallow.

"That beer sure tasted good, but I don't want another one. If you see that feller that had the mule, could you let me know? I got to go now."

"Where's my money for that beer? That one wasn't on the house, Chappie."

Chappie dug in his pocket, pulled out some change, and laid it on the table, saying, "Here you are, you old skinflint."

Cranky just laughed as Chappie went out the door.

Wesford walked back to his house, and was about to open the front door when he heard his name called.

"Hey, Chappie! Hold on there!"

It was the elder Henberry waving to him as he came up the road to the creek.

Chappie waited in the front yard for Henberry to say what he had to say.

"Howdy, there, Chappie. I've been looking for you. We never got to talk the other morning; you took off without even saying hello, hardly. What I wanted to see you about is my brother, Obadiah. He wasn't there when you came by, I don't think, but he's been acting strange lately. On Thanksgiving Day he and his friends hardly even talked with the family. They just said they wanted to talk about something and they all went out to the barn right after dinner, and the friends left without even saying goodbye. And this morning he sneaked out early and came back a couple of hours later and told me he had to get back home, that he'd be leaving right after he had some dinner. I don't know what to think. When I left, Milt said he would keep an eye on him for me. I came to town looking for you. I think I need some help with him. Obie's uncontrollable at times."

"What can I do for you? It sounds like it's just a family squabble. Maybe he didn't like the accommodations, or food, or something, and decided to go home."

"I think it's more than that, Chappie. I think he's in trouble, and is running away from something. I don't believe him, when he tells me he's going back home."

"Maybe I ought to take a ride out there and have a talk with him, if you think it would help any."

"It would, I'm sure, if you could do that. I'm going on out to the Proudmire place. I'm thinking about buying his pig farm from him, or I'd go with you."

"That's all right. I got to take care of something here in town, and then I'll go see if I can talk with your brother, Jim."

"Would appreciate it."

Chappie watched Mr. Henberry start down the road out of town towards the east, then he went and saddled up Spottie, and rode him to Cal Fedderson's house. Instead of going in, he gave a yell that somebody would hear in there he hoped, "Hey Calvin, Cal! Come on out, I got to talk to you now."

Barbara opened the door and saw that it was Chappie still on his horse, and told Cal, "Come and see what the Colonel wants."

"Howdy, Cal. I got a favor to ask of you. Is Max and Freddy still here?" Chappie asked, as he approached.

"Freddy is, but Max is herding the Henberry cows today. Why?"

"I need you to get your guns and come along with me, and I'll explain on the way. We're going to Esther's old house. Tell Barbara not to worry, you're going to help me kill a couple of pigs or something."

They started back to the house, and Chappie said, "I got a couple of prisoners tied up in there, and I need someone to guard them while I take a ride. Just don't let them loose. One of them was grazed in the arm by a bullet, and needs it cleaned up, but don't untie him or take any chances. They're both hard cases, so be careful. They're tied to the stove right now."

"How long you going to be gone?" asked Cal.

"I hope to be back before supper. Send Freddie for help, if you think you need it."

They reached the house and went in. The prisoners were still there securely tied to the stove.

"Well, gentlemen," said Chappie, "I've brought you some company to watch over you and take care of you while I'm gone. Cal, this is Rye and Flood."

Cal had a six-gun and a rifle, and Freddie was holding a rifle aimed at the crooks.

"We'll keep a close eye on them. You better get going," said Cal.

Chappie went outside, hopped on Spottie and headed out of town toward the Six-Mile Road. He was about a quarter-mile away from the trail used by the Henberrys to get to the dairy barn when he saw a rider coming through the cut in the hills. Chappie quickly directed Spottie off the road and into the cedar trees and sagebrush and hoped the rider hadn't seen him.

He tied Spottie to a cedar tree, hunkered down in the sagebrush, and watched the rider. "That's that Eddie Jensen. Must be going home or to town," he thought. Chappie watched as he came up the road, and, as he went by saw that he was holding something in one hand that looked like a book. He was concentrating so much on the book that he didn't look one way or another and was soon out of sight around a curve. Chappie returned his attention to the trail that led to the dairy barn.

"I hope my hunch is correct," Chappie murmured aloud. "If not, I'm wasting a lot of time."

He was about ready to give up when he spotted another lone rider coming into his line of vision on the trail. Chappie stood up and moved close to Spottie.

"I think that's that feller Bernie. Where's he going? And he's got bags over his saddlebags and his bedroll? Planning to leave the country, I'll bet," Chappie said to himself. "Hold on there. He's not getting on the road but behind the trees like I am. We'll just wait here for a minute or two and see what happens."

Spottie began pawing through the snow looking for something to eat, and Chappie held the reins so the horse wouldn't make any noise. Bernie or whoever it was, had hunkered down in the foliage and was barely visible.

"What's he doing, waiting for somebody, or just killing time?" Chappie wondered, as he kept an eye out for anyone coming along the road. He relaxed with one hand on Spottie's neck and shoulder, and stood very quietly trying not to make any noise. After awhile, he had to hunker down to a more comfortable position and look through the branches of the tree to see Bernie.

Chappie pulled a watch out of a pocket and saw that he had been hiding here almost two hours. But someone was coming up the road in a big hurry. He didn't recognize the horse or the rider as he slowed down approaching the trail. He replaced the watch in the pocket, as Bernie stood up, then walked out to the road and waved his arms. The rider slowed his horse to stop and said something to Bernie, who turned around and retrieved his horse from the cedar trees, then hopped on and the two were soon racing toward town.

Chappie hurriedly mounted Spottie and directed him out into the road, and by that time, the two riders were only about fifty to seventy-five yards away, and were charging fast. The two riders saw him and pulled up to a slower pace, and stopped when they were about fifteen or twenty feet away from Chappie.

"You fellers are in an awful big hurry today, aren't you?" asked Chappie.

"We got to get to town fast. We heard young Jim was in trouble there," said Obadiah. "You mind moving out of our way, Marshal, so we can get past."

"Howdy, Marshal. Fancy running into you again so soon. Where's Rye and Flood, if you don't mind me asking?" said Bernie.

"You must be Uncle Obadiah that old Jim was telling me about. I wanted to talk to you, too," Chappie said.

"What did Jim have to say, as if I cared?" asked Obie.

"Well, he wasn't very complimentary, for one thing. Said you were the black sheep of the family and always in trouble, even done some time for robbery of some sort. That true?"

"Might be. But, it's none of your business. Move your animal, we got to get going."

"Got a couple more questions for you. What've you got in your bags? Looks like a lot of supplies to be helping Jim with."

Bernie hadn't said anything up to now. He pulled his gun, aimed it the Marshal and said, "Get out of the road, or I'm going to blast you!"

"What're you doing, Bernie?" asked Obie. "You're crazy to pull your gun on the law," he said, and pulled his own gun.

But Chappie fell off Spottie away from the two, pulled his gun and shot them both, before they could even react. Bernie got hit in the right arm below the elbow, a glancing shot, and Obie got it in the right thigh. They both let out a cry, "A-a-g-g-h-h!" Obie got off a shot just before he was plugged, but it went skyward. He leaned over to grab his leg, fell off his horse and was lying in the road next to Bernie, moaning loudly, "Oh-oo, oh-ooo! I think I'm a goner! Uff-oh!"

Bernie stood up and looked for his artillery, but couldn't see it lying in the weeds by the road. "Where's my gun? What'd you do with it?"

"Help Obie get up! He's having a hard time, it looks like," ordered Chappie. "You fellers ought to know better than pulling your guns on a lawman. That's enough right there to put you away for a long time."

"Obie's hurt real bad in the leg. We better get him to a doctor afore he dies."

"He should've thought of that before he pulled his gun. Where's the bank money? In his saddlebags?"

"I don't know anything about any money. Get us to a doctor; we're losing a lot of blood. Oh-ooooo," Bernie said, letting out a long moan.

"There's plenty of time for that. Can't you get him to his feet?" said Chappie, grabbing the reins of Obie's horse and pulling off the saddlebags.

He ripped open a saddlebag and pulled out a small sack, opened it and poured some gold dust out into his palm.

"Well, well, well. It looks I've hit a goldmine. The money from the Price bank robbery, I'll bet."

"Leave...that....alone," Obie managed to say from his position on the ground.

"He's alive, and I think he might live. Get up, Obie! Help him to his feet, Bernie."

"He shot us both, Obie, and found the money. We might as well give up," said Bernie.

Chappie heard a horse coming along the road in the direction of the Henberry mill, and looked that way to see Milt loping toward them.

All three stood watching Milt approach, Bernie holding Obie up and Chappie still with the bag of gold dust. The Marshal poured the dust in his hand back in the bag, cinched it tight, and put it back in the saddlebag. He pulled his pistol and aimed it at the two wounded men.

"Don't go trying anything funny or you're done for. Milt's going to help me haul you two down to the valley," he said.

"Hey, Milt, look what this feller did to us for no reason. I think I'm dying. Can you help me get to a doctor? Look, we're bleeding to death."

"Well, Uncle Obie, it sure looks like you got yourself in to something this time, don't it? I'm not too sorry, though, 'cause I always knew you were no good."

"Let's throw him across his horse and take him to town. Come on, Obie, let's go," ordered the Marshal.

"Your killing me! Uf-f, a-ow-ooo!" Obie cried.

"Tie his hands and legs together under the belly. Bernie, I'm going to tie you up and help you get mounted. And don't try to run away or you'll be pulled off the horse."

"Aargh, ow-oo! Take it easy, Marshal, I got a hole in that arm! Aw-w-w," yelled Bernie as he was tied up and helped astride his horse.

The lawmen took them into town and held them overnight with Flood and Rye. The next morning they headed to the valley with all four prisoners, leaving town before daylight. There was a light snow falling as they passed the Bishop's store, and it was starting out to be dreary and cold, and it was going to be a long, gray, cold trip.

Cranky was up, getting an armload of wood for the fire he was going to make, and cussing Long John and Flat Paul for not loading his wood box after chopping all that wood. He heard the commotion of the Marshal and Milt getting the prisoners ready to travel. There were a lot of loud moans and groans coming from the back of the house as they loaded the prisoners onto their horses and began the trek out of town. He watched them as they passed the old saloon, and kept staring until they had passed out of sight in the falling snow, thinking, "It's going to be quiet around here without them two. I wonder when they'll be back."

And that old man Henberry had to give up on his plans to take over the town after his brother was captured. Everybody in town just knew he had ulterior motives and talked among themselves to destroy any chances he thought he had. Soon, all the farmers around started taking their grain and milk to the valley, even though it caused them excessive hardship to carry all that freight by wagon, but "that ole Henberry wasn't going to get any of my business, no sir," they said, and it ended up forcing Henberry to move elsewhere, lock, stock and barrel. Cal Fedderson saw an opportunity to make a little money by hauling that freight, and joined in a partnership with his brother-in-law, Roger Proudmire, after all they had been through. But that young Henberry feller, Oakley, stayed in Altaveel, married Hilaine Fedderson and settled right down, eventually re-opening the old grist mill for awhile before everybody had to find other places to live. Congress told the Indians they could have their land back, so everybody had to relocate, and the town of Altaveel is no more.